TAKE TWO

TAKE TWO

I HEART SAPPHFIC PRIDE COLLECTION

TB MARKINSON
MIRANDA MACLEOD

Copyright © 2022 T. B. Markinson & Miranda MacLeod

Cover Design by Victoria Cooper

Edited by Kelly Hathaway

This book is copyrighted and licensed for your personal enjoyment only. All rights reserved. No part of this publication may be reproduced, stored in a retrieval system, or transmitted in any forms or by any means without the prior permission of the copyright owner. The moral rights of the authors have been asserted.

This book is a work of fiction. Names, characters, businesses, places, events, and incidents are the product of the authors' imagination or are used fictitiously. Any resemblance to actual persons, living or dead, events, or locales is entirely coincidental.

CHAPTER ONE

Gina glanced up from the paper she was grading and nearly jumped out of her skin as she spied the head of the film studies department—in other words, the big boss—lurking in the office doorway.

"Professor Harlowe!" Gina worked to smooth the alarm from her face and voice. "Is there something I can do for you? Although, I have the Pride Festival committee meeting in five minutes, so…" She let her words trail off as way of saying, *hit the bricks, buddy*.

Instead of taking the hint and moving along, Evan Harlowe craned his neck to take a gander at the pile of papers on Gina's desk like she had all the time in the world to chitchat with him. While he was head of the department, he never seemed in a particular rush. It always made Gina wonder how he'd become so successful. Maybe it was a generational thing, with him having the good fortune of climbing the ladder before the concept of a *side hustle* came into being. Or that being a man meant he had less to prove by impersonating a perpetual motion machine.

"How's the grading coming?" he asked.

Gina's eyes slid to the stack of midterm exams in front of her. She forced a smile as she replied, "Great. Almost done."

In truth, the ratio of graded to ungraded papers was exactly the opposite of what she needed it to be. This meant her only hope for not pulling all-nighters for the next week was for today's meeting of the Comstock College Pride Festival planning committee, for which she'd somehow been suckered into serving as faculty liaison, would wrap up in record time.

Yeah, right.

The small group of undergrads she'd been tasked with herding since September could turn something as simple as choosing balloons into a debate worthy of the United Nations. With only two months to go until the big event, the likelihood of a drama-free afternoon seemed slim to nonexistent.

"And the Queer Power documentary?" The professor's lips became pinched. "You know we're expected to showcase the fifteen-minute trailer at the VIP reception at the Pride Festival. Will we be ready—"

"I've got it under control." As with the exam situation, this, too, was a stretch of the truth, but one Gina fully intended to rectify, even if she had to swear off sleep for a month and set up an IV with a caffeine drip directly into her veins.

Of course, it would be going a lot faster if the entire post-production of the two-hour film they were both supposed to be working on hadn't been dumped solely onto Gina's already overburdened shoulders. But she couldn't exactly say that part out loud. This would be her sixth year as an assistant professor under Evan Harlowe's guiding hand, and if she wanted her application for tenure to be approved at her next review, she needed to keep her mouth shut and meet her deadlines, however unreasonable they might seem.

Dr. Harlowe had just opened his mouth to continue speaking when a sudden ruckus outside the room caught him short. "What on earth?"

"That would be the committee—" Gina started to explain, but the professor was already making a hasty retreat. Gina couldn't really blame him. She might've done the same if that option were available to her.

The echoes of approaching mayhem sent Gina's hopes for an early evening plummeting. She couldn't tell what the students were talking about, but if she could hear them from this far down the hall, it didn't bode well. She affixed what she hoped was a neutral expression on her face, though anything less than murderous would be a win.

Destiny, a freshman with expressive brown eyes and rows of short, neat braids, was first to arrive. "Professor Mitchells, we're screwed."

"What?" Before Gina could fully process the unorthodox greeting, the young woman had thrust her phone a few inches from Gina's nose. Gina pulled back, blinking to avoid going cross-eyed. "What is this all about?"

"Lucas Brown." Destiny's voice wobbled, and for a moment, it seemed like she was about to burst into tears.

"The grand marshal of this year's Pride Parade?" Gina clarified as an uneasy tickle started in her belly, spreading like ants marching toward her extremities.

"Ex-grand marshal," said Kayla, a sophomore, who had entered Gina's office with two seniors in tow. Her freckled cheeks burned an alarming shade of crimson, and the matching fire in her eyes suggested the cause was anger rather than exertion.

Gina might've written it off as the typical drama of the committee's two youngest members, but the expressions on the older students' faces were equally grim. "Someone's going to need to explain from the beginning."

Destiny pressed play on the video she'd already cued on her phone, holding it further away this time so Gina could see the screen. It appeared to be a clip from Lucas Brown's comedy show, which Gina was vaguely aware had been held on campus over the weekend.

As soon as the audio started, Gina's jaw dropped.

"Did he just say the phrase *feminazi* on the campus of one of the oldest women's colleges in the country?"

"Keep watching," Kayla muttered.

Given the poor quality of the video, it was difficult to hear every word, but the dude's twisted smile and defiant pose filled in enough of the blanks for Gina to know Destiny's initial assessment was correct. They were screwed.

"Is there any chance all of that was staged as a practical joke?" Gina asked when the clip ended, fighting the urge to run to the bathroom so she could throw up. "Or is it too much to hope he was in the middle of a medical emergency?"

Like a stroke, for instance. That could account for the monumentally idiotic stream of hate-filled nonsense she'd just listened to, right? But the guy was only in his thirties, and it sure didn't look like he was having a stroke. No, he was simply going on a misogynistic, homophobic rant, and gobbling up every hiss and boo the audience produced in response.

"I'm confused," said Megan, a lanky senior with a buzzed head and nose ring, summing up what had to be the general feeling of the room with their clipped British accent. "I thought he was gay. Isn't that why we asked him to be grand marshal in the first place?"

That and he's cheap, Gina couldn't help but think. Sure, everyone loved the college's annual Pride Festival, but it didn't mean anyone was willing to fork over more money for it than they had to.

"He's totally gay," replied another student. "Gayer than gay."

Gina snorted before she had a chance to stop herself. As a femme-presenting, queer woman of color, she was especially sensitive to the need to avoid judging people by appearances. On the other hand, Lucas Brown was famously the most stereotypical caricature of a gay man she could possibly imagine. His flamboyant public persona made vintage Elton John look subdued by comparison. She never would've pegged him for the new poster child of the alt-right.

Which was what made judging by appearances so dangerous.

"Apparently, he's not gay anymore," Destiny said loudly with a vigorous shake of her head, hands firmly on her hips. "He's calling himself an ex-gay now."

"Did he agree to be our grand marshal because he's got a political agenda?" Kayla demanded. "Maybe he thinks he can show the women folk who's really in charge."

"Uh, excuse me," Megan interjected. "Not everyone here identifies as a woman. Do I need to remind you of my pronouns?"

"No, sorry," Kayla was quick to say, a look of chagrin on her face.

"I don't know what Lucas Brown wants, and I don't care." Destiny crossed her arms. She enunciated each word like she was heading into battle. "There's no way

I'm going to introduce that man as the grand marshal of our Pride Parade. No way at all."

As the room erupted into twenty opinions at once—quite a feat considering there were nowhere near that many present—Gina groaned. This was the last thing she needed on her agenda for the day.

"Hey!" Gina called out, making exactly zero dent in the cacophony surrounding her. She tried again, twice as loud. "Hey! We need to focus, people. It's only seven weeks until the festival. If we're going to invite a new grand marshal, we need to decide that today."

"There's no choice." Kayla flicked her hands in the air for emphasis. "Already, one band has threatened to pull out. Vendors are emailing me, seeking clarification as to whether Lucas is still involved, and threatening to walk if the answer is yes."

"We're ruined," Destiny exclaimed. "Sunk. Dead in the water."

"We don't know that for sure." Gina silently added the word *yet*, because the way the internet worked these days, the clip was already being viewed by penguins in the Antarctic. Repercussions would be swift.

"Who can we get to step in at such a late stage?" Megan's gaze met everyone in the room in turn. "If you asked me to do it, especially knowing who I was replacing, I wouldn't want to be anywhere near the stink. Would you?" Again, their gaze challenged everyone, finally resting on Gina.

With a sinking feeling, Gina realized they were all waiting on her to solve the problem with the wave of a magic wand.

"You teach film studies." Destiny offered up her best puppy dog eyes. "Surely you know someone famous."

"I make documentaries," Gina corrected. "About the experiences of underrepresented racial, ethnic, queer, and gendered identities. I don't have Jodie Foster's phone number. If I did, I would've tried that before we saddled ourselves with a guy like Lucas Brown."

"It's so unfair," Destiny moaned. "The Hasty Pudding Club at Harvard never has to scrape the bottom of the barrel for support. They snap their fingers, and celebrities come running. We have to settle for D-list comedians."

"We're not going to settle," Gina stated with as much confidence as she could muster. Someone needed to show leadership, and sadly, she was the one nominally in charge of this three-ring circus.

With that in mind, she rose to her feet, setting her nearly forgotten red grading pen on her desktop with a loud thud. "I am going down the hall to refill my water bottle. While I'm doing that, I want Megan to pull up the list we made in September of possible grand marshals. Let's see if any of them are viable options. The rest of you, start brainstorming new ideas. Be creative."

In the relative silence of the deserted hallway, Gina wondered how necessary it was that she use the closest water fountain for her task. The one downstairs in the faculty break room would take her away from the chaos for twice as long. The one across campus in the science department sounded even better. With a sigh, she opted for the closest one, but gave herself permission to stop in the restroom on her way back. It was late in the afternoon, and there was a good chance her mascara was starting to flake.

Can't have that.

As it turned out, her makeup, what little she wore, didn't need touching up. Even her lipstick was too fresh to waste time on. Fresh out of excuses, Gina trudged back to the meeting. When she entered the room, a disagreement was already in progress and growing more heated by the second.

"That is like *so* bi-phobic," Kayla declared hotly, presumably at Megan, who had their hands balled into fists and looked ready to spit.

"Only because you're twisting what I said," Megan shouted back.

"I am not—"

"All right. Enough!" Gina sucked in a breath, unable to shake the feeling she'd been channeling her mother just then. Not the person she ever wanted to be. "I want a calm, rational explanation of what the problem is."

"I found the perfect candidate for grand marshal,

and Megan is being their stubborn self about it, as always."

"Kayla," Gina warned.

"Sorry, but I just found out an actor with ties to Massachusetts, who identifies as bisexual—"

"But has never been photographed in the company of anyone but her hunky co-stars," Megan interjected.

"Nope." Gina held up a hand as she shook her head, perhaps a little more fiercely than she would have had it not been for the lingering guilt over snorting about Lucas Brown being gayer than gay. "You know better than that, Megan. We've talked about it in here a million times, but it bears repeating. Your sexuality is not defined by who you're dating."

"For normal people, yeah," Megan countered. "But I'm so sick of fake celebrities jumping on the rainbow train for some extra attention on social media."

"There's no reason to think—" Kayla began.

This time Gina cut off Kayla. "Look, unless anyone here knows this woman personally, I don't think this is a matter we can settle right now, okay? But I'm intrigued. What makes you think we could get her to agree to be grand marshal?"

Kayla flashed a triumphant smile in Megan's direction before turning back to Gina, who could've sworn she'd wandered into a roomful of preschoolers instead of college students. "According to social media, she's going to be filming a movie—"

"One of those cishet, made-for-cable, Christmas

movies," Megan seemed compelled to add. "With all the red and green sweaters."

Gina's heart stalled for the length of a beat. A Christmas movie starring a local actor? No, it couldn't be. The *Queen of Christmas* filmed all her movies in Canada. It had to be a coincidence. Many actors made a living making holiday movies, not just... her.

"I love those movies," Destiny said, looking like she might be ready to start yet another fight.

"She's filming a movie..." Gina prompted, shutting her eyes and wondering how many more minutes she could go before her brain thudded its way right out of her skull.

"On location," Kayla continued, "about twenty minutes from here. And according to the article, the shoot lasts until the end of May, so she'll definitely be around for the festival. Oh, and this is good news. According to one of her fan groups, the type who border on stalking, she's already in town."

The room went silent, and Gina held her breath, waiting for someone else to jump in, but no one did. As she dared to open her eyes a crack, she discovered that all the committee members were watching her, clearly waiting for her to weigh in. Gina ran through what Kayla had suggested, finding it surprisingly promising. For the first time since the meeting had started, her shoulders loosened a smidge.

"Okay. That doesn't sound like a half-bad option." When Megan made a growling sort of cough as she rolled her eyes to the ceiling, Gina rounded on her, not willing to start this all over again. "Do you have a better idea?"

"No, but it's just so embarrassing," Megan grumbled.

"Worse than an ex-gay Rush Limbaugh wannabe?" Gina challenged, folding her arms in victory when Megan stayed silent. "I didn't think so. Like it or not, we're not Harvard, and we can't snap our fingers and make Oscar-winning actors do our bidding. The woman's got a local connection, she's part of the LGBTQ+ community—and you know what? I like those Christmas movies, too. Even if they are mostly about straight white people in ugly sweaters baking cookies no one seems to eat, which is a crime in my book."

This was one hundred percent true, even if she hadn't been able to bring herself to watch one in years. Gina would never have admitted to anything so counter to her intellectual image if it was a lie. Even so, airing her dirty secret in front of her students made her wish she could climb under her desk and disappear.

"So, we should go for it?" Kayla's eyes widened, a smile spreading across her face. "Everyone who agrees we should reach out and invite Sophia Rossi to be the grand marshal of this year's Pride Parade, raise your hand."

"What?" Gina went ice cold so quickly at the

confirmation they were indeed pitching Sophia Rossi—the *Queen of Christmas* herself—it was like she'd been dipped in a vat of liquid nitrogen. "No."

"Huh?" Kayla's face scrunched, and even Megan looked confused.

"No, we can't..." Gina stopped to clear her throat, suddenly aware of a weird cackling laugh that was apparently coming from her own mouth. "I'm sorry, but we can't invite Sophia Rossi to be part of our festival."

"See?" Megan gave Kayla a smug look. "I told you. That woman is a total fake. No way she's bisexual."

Oh, God. Gina was on the verge of hyperventilating. *There's that horrible laugh again.*

Everyone was staring at her with the type of alarm in their eyes that suggested they were weighing whether or not to call an ambulance. With supreme effort, Gina pulled together whatever scraps of her sanity she could.

"I assure you, her sexuality is *not* the problem." Gina's volume was barely above a whisper.

Megan let out an exasperated breath. "You're only saying that because—"

"Because I know." This time, Gina's voice was nearly back to normal, though that was about the only part of her that was. The rest was shaking like a tub of Jell-O after an earthquake. "I did say earlier we could settle the matter if anyone here knew her."

"*You* know Sophia Rossi?" Destiny blurted. "The Keynote Channel's biggest holiday romance star?"

"Yeah." Gina closed her eyes again, this time wishing the action would make her disappear. "Which is how I know she'll never agree to be the grand marshal."

"Why not?" asked Kayla.

"Because…" Gina dug her nails into her palms, hoping the pain would help her maintain consciousness. "Because Sophia Rossi was my college girlfriend. I broke up with her on graduation day, and she vowed to hate me until she died."

CHAPTER TWO

Sophia emerged from her rental car, blinking into the early morning sun. She clutched a cup of hot coffee to her chest like it contained a lifesaving elixir. Which, considering it was still three-quarters full of dark roast with extra milk, it basically did.

What she could see of downtown Sholan Falls looked exactly like it had since she was a kid, right down to the definitely not licensed images of Disney cartoon characters that had been painted in the window of the local travel agency by an amateur artist decades ago. The single screen movie theater was still there, too, where she and Gina had kissed for the first time that holiday break their sophomore year when Gina had come home with her because she was on the outs with her parents over the whole *lesbian* thing.

A strange feeling came over Sophia, like she'd

fallen through a crack in time. Any minute now, Gina would come running across the common, grabbing her hand to lead her to the candy shop with its glass case of homemade truffles, or the independent bookstore with the friendly black cat in the window, just as she had that weekend so long ago. Sophia swigged a mouthful of coffee to ground herself in reality again. Gina was long gone, and probably a million miles away, pursuing a life that had no room in it for Sophia.

Gina had made that perfectly clear.

Ten years away would have made many places in the world completely unrecognizable, but not this little corner of rural Massachusetts. Sholan Falls was Sophia's hometown. As far as she could see, not much had changed since the day she'd left.

She'd find out for sure next weekend, which was when her mother *thought* Sophia would be arriving in town—because that was what Sophia had led her mom to believe. This movie—her first under a new contract with International Broadcasting Conglomerate that was easily worth ten times what the Keynote Channel had been paying her, along with a producer credit—was too big a deal. No way could she afford the distraction of her huge Italian-American family descending on her while she was still trying to establish her footing and get through a week of table reads and costume fittings.

For now, Sophia was keeping a low profile. That was a fancy way of saying she was hiding from anyone who might recognize her from way back when. Luckily, film sets were kept secure, and the majority of her work would be indoors this week, so the chance of being discovered was minimal. Staying hidden until her call time would've been the safest bet, but that was taking the subterfuge too far.

Plus, she simply couldn't contain her curiosity at seeing a film crew in her hometown, something she daydreamed about as a child.

Sophia wasn't expected for several hours, but she was like a child on Christmas morning, and she couldn't resist seeing what was going on first hand. Though the crew was still hard at work, half of Main Street had already been transformed into a magical Christmas village nicer than anything the town had ever enjoyed in real life.

"Move it or lose it!" a man barked, carrying a plank past Sophia at breakneck speed in a manner that was anything but holly jolly.

"Oh, sorry," she mumbled, changing direction to scramble to one of the only small patches of green in the town common that was free of cables, cords, or building supplies.

Immediately, a man with thick brown hair and round cheeks, clutching a clipboard with a very official air, made a beeline for her. "Excuse me, ma'am. You aren't supposed to be—wait, Ms. Rossi?" The man scrunched his face, sending his black-framed glasses high onto the bridge of his nose. "What are you doing on set already? Your call time isn't until this afternoon."

"I know, but I—" Sophia stopped mid-sentence, the man's face suddenly clicking in her memory. "Hold on. Matt Pasini? Is that you?"

"Uh, yeah… gosh." A ferocious blush bloomed on his cheeks as he donned a deer in headlights expression. "I was sure you wouldn't remember me."

"Goodness, what are the odds? You were a freshman in the St. Cecelia High School drama club my senior year, right?" Sophia couldn't control her silly grin, overcome by the coincidence of running into someone she knew. She should have anticipated it, considering at one point in her life she'd probably known half the town, but none of them were movie folks. Plus, the executive producer, who had also recently defected from the Keynote Channel, preferred to bring all his own people wherever he filmed. It had never occurred to her any of the locals would be involved.

"We did *The Sound of Music* together," Matt reminisced. "You were the most amazing Maria," he added with something akin to awe in his tone.

"As I recall, the way you sang Kurt's line in *So Long, Farewell*—wearing your lederhosen with those chubby cheeks you had back then—brought the house down every night." Sophia chuckled, noting silently that the man's cheeks were still round, but he'd mostly grown into them as an adult.

"Wow, you really *do* remember."

"Of course, I do. I was jealous over how adorable you were," Sophia confessed. "No way could I compete. It's funny. My memory's terrible now for anything but the lines I need to know for the day, but the tiniest details from my acting past are lodged in my brain forever."

Including the stuff I'd rather forget, a little voice in her head whispered, but Sophia pushed it aside and vowed never to cyber-stalk her ex. She wouldn't allow herself to dwell on bad times when things were really looking up.

"Well, I sure haven't forgotten you," Matt admitted shyly. "You were always really nice to all of us younger students, even though it was clear way back then you'd go on to be a star and eclipse the rest of us."

"Oh, yes," Sophia scoffed. "I'm the *Queen of Christmas*. That's one step away from being Marilyn Monroe. Or, like, the actual queen."

"Hey, don't mock it. Everyone in town has been talking about this movie, not to mention you and Butch, like you're gods."

Ah, yes. Butch.

That was another element that had followed her from the Keynote Channel. They'd starred in at least half a dozen movies together, and considering this film was IBC's first foray into the lucrative Christmas movie market, the network had been thrilled to sign them both. It was fine. They got along well enough, even went to premieres and studio events together sometimes. If Sophia had been hoping for a bit bigger of a change with her move to a new company, she still wasn't going to complain. Why mess with a winning formula?

"What's your role with the production?" Sophia asked, happy enough to move the attention off of herself and get out of her own head. "Not an actor, or at least that's what I'm gathering from the clipboard in your hand and that very impressive headset you've got on."

"I'm a production assistant." Matt's voice burst with pride. "I studied stage management at Boston University and worked at some smaller theaters in the area, but this is my first time working on a film."

"This production is twice the size I'm used to, and double the filming days, too, so I'll be learning the ropes right beside you." Sophia jumped as a loud round of cursing erupted from the gazebo under construction on the other side of the town common. "Hey, that's new. I always thought this space would look nicer with a gazebo."

"*Half* the town agrees with you." Matt's arched eyebrow suggested there was much more to this story, and Sophia was there for it.

"Oh, do tell." She rubbed her hands together, knowing there was no better flavor of gossip than the small-town variety.

"Have you not heard about Gazebogate?" Matt

pressed a hand to his chest in mock surprise. "Surely, your mother would've told you about this scandal by now."

Sophia cringed at the mention of her mother. "I will deny this to my dying breath if you mention it to anyone, but it's possible I've been ghosting my mother a bit these past several weeks since I found out I got the part."

"Sophia Rossi!" Matt's mouth dropped open as he feigned shock at her confession. "Does she not know you're going to be here?"

"I'm not that good a liar," Sophia said quickly. "But I kinda told her I didn't get into town until Saturday instead of Wednesday. I couldn't help it. I need to focus, and she stresses me out with all her questions, and her—what am I saying? I remember your mom from the cafeteria in elementary school. The two of them could be twins."

"True, which is why I'm the last person to judge," Matt assured her with utmost sincerity. "Although I was going to give you all sorts of respect if you could pull off hiding your presence in Sholan Falls for two months."

"Heck no. Mom's got some sort of kid radar. She'd sniff me out like a bloodhound. Normally, I wouldn't lie to her at all." Sophia clenched her hands, the very thought of what she'd done putting her nerves on edge. "But in addition to this being my first film with IBC, my little sister's getting married this summer, and my older sister's pregnant. Mom's need to know when I plan to get married and produce offspring will be in hyperdrive."

Matt offered a thoughtful nod. "Maybe she'll just be happy to see you and proud of your significant professional accomplishments."

There was silence as a second or two ticked past; after which, they both burst into side-splitting guffaws.

"Yeah, right," Sophia gasped. "That's a good one."

"Can you imagine?" Matt howled, laughing so hard tears spilled from his eyes. "I take it there's no fiancé waiting back at the inn to surprise her with. Unless the rumors about you and Butch are true?"

"Not remotely, you cheeky monkey," Sophia teased. "I don't have time for a goldfish, let alone a relationship."

The denial about being involved with Butch was dead-on, but the second part was only partially true.

Her schedule was crazy, sure. Filming outside of Vancouver much of the year between trips back home to LA would put a crimp in anyone's social calendar. But Sophia's heart was the real culprit behind her single status.

From the moment they'd met, Gina Mitchells had been the only person for Sophia. They'd planned a whole life together after graduation, moving to LA so Gina could write screenplays and Sophia could act. But when the time had come, Gina had all but given her a swift kick in the ass, making it clear in that moment that Sophia wasn't good enough for Gina's ambitious life plan.

That knowledge had shattered her heart into a million tiny pieces that could never be put back together again. No, worse. Her heart had been set alight, burned to a crisp, and ground to fine, dusty powder. There was nothing left of the thing except the dull ache in her chest where her heart had once been.

Explaining this to a guy she'd last seen as a pimply-faced high school freshman wearing lederhosen seemed a bit over the top.

As Sophia struggled for an escape from this conversation, her eyes fell on the charming white structure that was rapidly taking shape on the grassy town square. "You still haven't told me what the thing is with the gazebo."

"You won't believe it," Matt assured her, all talk of significant others seemingly forgotten. "Well, since you grew up in Sholan Falls, you might. Our town was the perfect location to film in, except for one thing. It lacked a gazebo."

"Christmas movie towns must have gazebos," Sophia commented, having become an expert on the genre after starring in no fewer than twenty holiday flicks. "Everyone knows that."

"Exactly, and it's an easy fix. We're building one, like a quality one, not a prop. It's made out of good wood and everything." Matt gestured toward the partially finished structure, and Sophia could see for herself how nice it looked. "The deal is, after we wrap, we're leaving the gazebo in place. It can't be taken apart without destroying it."

"It would be a waste to tear it down," Sophia opined. "And this might be the only New England town that didn't already have one. Seems like a win."

"Oh, definitely," Matt agreed. "Like I said before, half the town is thrilled."

"And the other half?" Sophia was already holding back laughter. Even without knowing the details, she could guess whatever she was about to hear would be deliciously ridiculous. As she'd already noted, nothing much had changed in these parts, including small town drama.

"The other half is wicked pissed," Matt explained, sucking in his cheeks in what seemed to be an effort to hold in his own laughter. "The historical society claims it's an eyesore to have a gazebo with an architectural style from the 1910s while the downtown buildings were erected in the 1850s."

"Are you serious?" Sophia's eyes darted to the perfectly lovely gazebo. "Is the town paying for it?"

"Not a dime, but Helen with the historical society is our resident mean girl, and in the end, people love to bitch about anything—" Matt's eyes doubled in size as something behind Sophia caught his attention. "No! No! No!"

"What is it?" Sophia demanded as her head

whipped toward whatever had cause the production assistant such alarm. Her heart was racing even though she had no idea what the problem could be. It sounded serious.

"Excuse me, Soph." Formalities forgotten in the face of what had to be impending disaster, Matt stormed off without a backward glance, shouting, "We can't have red, white, and blue bunting! This is a frigging Christmas movie, not the Fourth of July!"

Sophia chuckled as she raised her coffee to her mouth. Her town was the same as always, all right. Although, as two crew members unfurled a giant roll of cotton batting to serve as snow beneath a massive fake Christmas tree, it was rapidly becoming unrecognizable, too. And surreal. The forecast called for seventy degrees that afternoon, unseasonably warm for early April. Although compared to all those middle of summer shoots she'd endured with Keynote, only sweating a little bit in her costume would be a delight.

As if channeling her younger self playing the role of Maria, Sophia spread her arms wide and spun in a slow, deliberate circle. She needed to take it all in, but as the details overwhelmed her, Sophia closed her eyes.

This feels like a dream.

When she'd come to a stop and opened her eyes again, a woman stood in front of her, with flawless dark skin and an abundant head of curls so unchanged since the last time Sophia had seen her that she was even more convinced she was dreaming. She'd had this dream a thousand times since graduation, only each time it ended up more like a nightmare, with Gina telling her she wasn't good enough and walking away while Sophia sobbed in her cap and gown.

Despite the sweat that had begun to bead at the base of her hairline from the intense morning sun, Sophia shivered. The coffee cup she still held in one hand slipped from her grasp and smashed to the ground, spraying droplets all over Sophia's feet.

The burn of hot liquid against her bare ankles jolted Sophia from her trance. "What the fuck, Gina?"

As her ex's expression morphed from hesitance to shock, Sophia realized this definitely wasn't a dream. For one thing, in her dreams, Sophia usually came up with a more appropriate greeting. Although the one she'd barked out certainly seemed to be having an impact. Gina appeared on the verge of turning tail and running away.

"I shouldn't have come." Gina was breathless to the point that Sophia feared she might pass out.

Before Gina could flee, Sophia reached for her arm and held her in place. "Oh no you don't. I want to know what you're doing here before you scram."

"It's stupid. I'm sorry." In all their years together, Sophia couldn't recall seeing the usually unflappable Gina so flustered. Not even the day she'd dumped her. Maybe especially not then. "I was going to ask a favor, but—"

"You wanted to ask *me* a favor?" Sophia couldn't believe she'd heard that right.

Gina shook her head. "Like I said, it was a mistake. I should just—"

"There's my baby girl!" Even coming from all the way on the other side of the town common, there was no mistaking that voice.

"Oh my God," Sophia whimpered, spotting the source of the greeting. "It's my mother." Apparently, security on the set wasn't fully operational yet. First Sophia's ex and now her mom. Who was next? The Easter Bunny?

"Your mother?" Gina's eyes widened, giving her the look of a terrified squirrel, as she, too, spotted the woman charging across the expanse of green, heading straight for them. "Oh shit."

"Right?" Sophia tightened her grip on Gina's arm, her brain whirling. One hour in town and her mother had already sniffed Sophia out. And now she'd know Sophia had lied to her, unless something really big happened to distract her. Like a meteorite the size that had wiped out the dinosaurs landing in the middle of Sholan Falls. *Or, maybe...* "You said you needed a favor?"

"Well, I—"

"Whatever it is, I'll do it." Sophia's words tumbled out in a whoosh, her heart racing as her mother yelled out her name again. Time was running out. "But you have to do something for me first."

"Yeah, okay." Gina had to have been as rattled as Sophia because she didn't even stop to ask what before agreeing to it.

"Whatever I say or do for the next fifteen minutes, play along." Sophia's entire body vibrated as adrenaline coursed through every vein.

"Do?" A little late, Gina seemed to be rethinking whatever it was she'd gotten herself into. "What are you planning to *do*?"

"This..." With no further warning, Sophia clasped Gina to her, smashing their lips together in a bruising kiss.

CHAPTER THREE

THE CRUSH OF SOPHIA'S DEMANDING MOUTH drove the air from Gina's lungs and all awareness from her brain, save for the rush of memories of every kiss they'd ever shared. Over the past ten years, Gina had convinced herself she'd exaggerated how good it felt to hold Sophia in her arms. All that hard work of self-deception was wiped out in less than a second. In truth, the reality was even better than Gina had remembered.

"I can't believe it!" Sophia's mom cried out.

Gina blinked away the fog in her eyes as Sophia released her lips and allowed their bodies to drift apart, though her ex maintained a vice-like grip on her arm, as though making sure Gina couldn't flee. Smart thinking. Considering what Mrs. Rossi must think of Gina after breaking up with Sophia the way she had, running for the hills held a huge appeal.

"Uh... Mrs. Rossi," Gina stuttered. Had there been anger in the woman's tone? Gina had been too distracted being kissed by the woman's daughter to notice. "Hi."

"You two are back together again?" Sophia's mother asked. Or was the question more of a demand? Gina was still unable to read the woman's mood. All she could think of was how soft and full Sophia's lips were, and how certain Gina had been she'd never experience that feeling again after how she'd treated Sophia ten years before.

For her own good, Gina reminded herself. But, still. Gina doubted Sophia saw it that way, which left one very important question.

What the hell had just happened?

"Mom," Sophia soothed, removing one hand from Gina's arm so she could use it to squeeze her mother's shoulder. Apparently, Sophia had taken it upon herself to keep both the women tethered to her, perhaps so no one would fly off the handle. "I can explain."

Gina tilted her head, dying to hear whatever story Sophia had concocted.

"And to think," Mrs. Rossi replied, a look of fondness softening her features, "I was coming over here to scold you, young lady, for sneaking into town without so much as a text."

"I know. I'm sorry, Mom. But... Gina and I wanted some alone time before our schedules got crazy."

Sophia threaded her fingers through Gina's, giving every digit a death squeeze.

As Mrs. Rossi redirected her gaze, Gina tensed, preparing to be read the riot act. At least now she understood why Sophia had kissed her. That was about the only thing shocking enough to divert Mrs. Rossi from the cardinal sin of a daughter not alerting her mother Sophia was in town.

But the fact it had been Gina, of all people, on the receiving end of those lips? No way would Mrs. Rossi stand for that. There would be consequences, and apparently, Gina would have to face them as payment for Sophia agreeing to the favor Gina had yet to formally ask.

But instead of a scowl, the older woman broke into a broad, toothy grin. "This is the most amazing news. I'm completely overcome." Mrs. Rossi waved a hand in front of her face, perhaps as a way of protecting her mascara from running, or she was winding up a sucker punch to Gina's face.

"It is?" Gina clutched Sophia's hand, grateful she'd yet to let go as it was suddenly the only thing keeping her upright. "You are?"

"Of course!" Mrs. Rossi gawked at them like they were part of a department store Christmas window. "I've been telling Sophia for years the two of you belong together like sugar and cinnamon. I'm grateful my fool of a daughter finally came to her senses."

Baffled, Gina opened her mouth to ask what was

going on. The way Mrs. Rossi made it sound, anyone would've thought Sophia had done the breaking up instead of Gina. As Sophia gave Gina's fingers another squeeze, she shot Gina a look that said *keep playing along, and I'll explain later*. Or maybe Mrs. Rossi's mind wasn't as sharp as it used to be, and it was only a matter of time until she remembered she hated Gina's guts.

Gina's pulse ticked faster, waiting for Mrs. Rossi's lightbulb moment.

"Do you forgive me for telling you I wasn't getting into town until the weekend?" Sophia asked her mom with such innocence that if Gina didn't already know how talented an actor the woman was, this would have been all the proof needed.

"Of course, I do." Mrs. Rossi pulled her daughter close enough to plant a kiss on the top of her head before offering Gina one of her warmest motherly smiles, the kind she'd missed so much that it immediately turned Gina's insides as gooey as one of Mrs. Rossi's freshly baked chocolate chip cookies. "Gina, how long are you here visiting from New York?"

"Oh… well…" Naturally, that was what Mrs. Rossi, and probably Sophia, assumed. It had been Gina's plan to move there and pursue a career in documentary film the last they'd known. But life hadn't worked out exactly how she'd plotted. "Funny thing, really. I recently moved back to the area."

If six years could be considered recent.

Mrs. Rossi let out another mom-type squeal. "I had no idea!"

For good reason. Gina made it a point never to step foot in Sholan Falls. Part of it was the bittersweet memories of time spent with Sophia in this place, which tugged at old wounds and threatened to open them wide. The other part was dreading the possibility of bumping into Sophia's mom, or her two sisters, or any member of the extended family. Beyond dreading condemnation from people she'd once loved, Gina feared falling down the rabbit hole of wondering if she'd made the worst mistake of her life in letting Sophia go.

"Now that the secret's out of the bag," Mrs. Rossi was saying, seemingly unaware that Gina hadn't responded, "you two must come to dinner tonight."

"Tonight?" Gina swallowed, her brain clawing at possible excuses to get out of saying yes.

"Yes, tonight." There was just enough steel in Sophia's tone, not to mention tension in that iron grip on Gina's arm her ex showed no signs of loosening, that Gina shut her mouth and nodded. After all, she'd promised to go along with anything Sophia said or did for fifteen minutes, and though it felt like an eternity, she was pretty sure if she'd had the ability to move her arm enough to check her watch, no more than five minutes had passed so far.

"Wonderful!" Mrs. Rossi clapped her hands together, beaming with such joy Gina was glad to have had a part in it. She would send her regrets later, of course, concocting a plausible emergency. Gina did have a lot of grading to do, but that didn't seem to tick the full-on emergency box for the likes of Mrs. Rossi. Nope, Gina would have to come up with something catastrophic, and based on Sophia's performance so far, she would certainly be able to sell it. Since dinner landed well outside the fifteen-minute window, Gina wouldn't have to feel guilty about canceling.

Just devastated.

"Mom, wouldn't you like a tour of the set?" Sophia asked, raising her free hand to wave at a man with a clipboard and thick spectacles who was picking his way through a pile of cables and cords. "Hey, Matt!"

The man looked over, straightening up when he spotted Sophia and trotting over with an eager to please expression.

"Matt, you remember my mom, don't you?" Sophia asked.

"Of course," he replied. "Everyone knows Mrs. Rossi's bakery makes the best cannoli in town."

"Wait, now—" Mrs. Rossi took a step back, her eyes growing huge as she looked the man up and down. "This can't be little Matt Pasini, can it?"

"All grown-up," he told her, stating the obvious.

"Matt's working as a production assistant on the film, Mom," Sophia said briskly, probably so her mom wouldn't have an opportunity to start strolling down memory lane. "I'm sure he'd love to take you around and show you everything." As Matt's face blanched, Gina knew from personal experience he was probably being run ragged and had real work to do, not babysit Mrs. Rossi. Sophia added in her most beguiling way, "Then he can introduce you to the right person to work out bringing over a big batch of cannolis to the set sometime. Wouldn't that be nice?"

"You bet!" The production designer's eyes lit up at the promise of cannoli like it was actually almost Christmas instead of just looking like it. "Follow me, Mrs. Rossi."

"That was smooth," Gina said once the two were out of earshot.

As if realizing they no longer had to put on a show, Sophia dropped Gina's hand like a lead balloon. "You have to come to dinner tonight."

"That was not part of the deal," Gina argued, panic rising as she realized it had been foolish to think this would continue to go as easily as it had seemed to in the beginning. Could they go back to the kissing?

Storm clouds settled deep into Sophia's dark brown eyes. "What exactly *is* this deal? I have no idea what I agreed to."

"I need you to be part of the Comstock College Pride Festival."

"Our alma mater?" A mix of surprise and confusion played across Sophia's features.

"I'm teaching there now," Gina explained, not

wanting to go into the details and risk revealing how poorly things had gone in New York. "So, you'll do it?"

Sophia rested a finger on her chin. "I just need to attend?"

"Well..." Gina cringed as she allowed herself to draw out the last syllable way longer than she'd intended. "I need you to be the grand marshal. It means having your picture and name used in the publicity, riding on a special float in the parade, and giving a quick speech at the event."

Sophia nodded, but much too slowly to be mistaken for agreement. Clearly, she was thinking it over, and no doubt looking either for a way out, or a way to get more out of Gina than the fifteen minutes she'd already given. "When is it?"

"Mid-May."

"Oh. I'll still be in town." Sophia slumped, and a feeling of triumph washed over Gina. It was short-lived as Sophia demanded, "Why don't you already have a grand marshal if the event is so close?"

"We, uh, did." Gina swallowed hard, balking at telling Sophia the whole story, but the look in Sophia's eyes said there was no way around it. "It was Lucas Brown."

"Oh, fuck." Sophia's response, especially considering she'd never been much for bad language in the past, made it unnecessary for Gina to ask if Sophia was aware of the comedian's recent dust-up. "I'm going to have to clear this with my publicist, the higher ups at IBC, and the producer on my film before I can—"

"We had a deal!" Gina dug her fingernails into her palms as her indignation mounted. Or was it fear? So much was riding on the Pride Festival going off without a hitch.

"I'm not backing out." Sophia put up a hand in a calming gesture. "But with Lucas Brown in the mix, this is bigger than I thought. The social media buzz is going to be through the roof, and if IBC is anything like the Keynote Channel, they may be skittish when it comes to LGBTQ+ stuff."

"Oh, great," Gina muttered. "Like it's my fault you sold your soul to some homophobic—"

"Stop right there," Sophia commanded, an undeniable tinge of anger in her words that caught Gina by surprise. "You have no idea what I've been through or what it's cost me to get to where I am right now. Know why? Because you left me to fend for my fucking self ten years ago. You don't get to judge."

Two fucks in one minute? That was bad. Really bad. No, wait. Sophia had said fuck when greeting Gina, if that could be called a greeting. So, it was much worse. Three fucks during one encounter.

"You're right," Gina rushed to placate. "I'm sorry. I'm in no position to say anything."

"It isn't easy to make it in Hollywood, Gina." Sophia's eyes shone with unshed tears that squeezed Gina's heart like a vice.

Even if she'd wanted to cast a stone or two, she was in no position to do it. If Sophia had sold her soul to the Keynote Channel, Gina wasn't much different in going to work for a mentor she knew would run her ragged and take all the credit. It turned out that was how the real world worked. Sometimes you had to compromise.

Other times, begging helped.

"I'm not asking for me, Soph." Gina said quietly. "My students are devastated by what Lucas did, and—"

"All right, all right, I get it." Sophia sighed, long and low. "I'll work it out on my end, whatever it takes. But this has definitely raised the bar, and I'm going to need something more from you."

"Fine. What are we talking, like, dinner tonight with your parents?" Gina tensed, pretty sure she would never survive such an ordeal, but what could she do? The students were counting on her, and without a grand marshal, the Pride Festival would bomb, which would be disastrous for her tenure review.

"Dinner's the least you can do. I don't think you grasp how much trouble this is going to be for me. I'm the *Queen of Christmas*. My fans love red and green, but they're not necessarily keen on rainbows." Sophia pretended to consider her terms, though Gina had a feeling she already knew exactly what she wanted. "While I'm in town for this job, for as long as I have to put up with my mom pestering me about my life, I need you to pretend we're dating. Do we have a deal?"

"It's not like I have a choice." Gina shut her eyes, wishing she'd never heard of Lucas Brown, Sholan Falls, and especially the Rossi family. She'd gotten what she'd come here for, but at what price? Gina had barely survived walking away from Sophia once. A second time might destroy Gina.

CHAPTER FOUR

When Sophia pulled up in front of the white two-story colonial house with the black shutters where she'd spent her childhood, Gina was already there, pacing the sidewalk in front of the neighbor's place.

"What are you doing?" Sophia demanded in a stage whisper as she exited her car. "Have you forgotten which house it is?"

Gina spun around, and Sophia's heart was pierced with a familiar ache at the sight of her ex. Sophia had spent hours working to make sure every hair was in place and all her flaws were well hidden. It was part of her job, no matter how fake it sometimes seemed. Meanwhile, Gina was the type who went through life unapologetically herself, with a natural beauty Sophia envied as much as she admired. And occasionally lusted after, even now.

"I haven't forgotten," Gina replied, her expression clouding with trepidation as her eyes landed on the Rossi house.

"Shall we?" Sophia asked lightly, holding out her arm. "My mom's probably happier to see you tonight than me."

"Come on." As she said this, Gina raised an eyebrow in a way that telegraphed *don't shit with me*. "Your whole family must hate me, considering the way I broke your heart."

"They probably would, if they knew." Sophia looked away, unable to face the sudden questioning in Gina's eyes

"What are you talking about?"

"The truth is, I told them I broke up with you." Sophia closed her eyes, bracing herself against the rush of hurt that still accompanied the memories of that terrible day.

"What?" There was no mistaking the disbelief in Gina's tone.

"Yeah. I told them you'd only hold me back in LA. You know, like what you said to me about going with you to New York after you woke up one day and decided instead of writing rom-coms, you preferred being a documentary filmmaker." Sophia grew defensive. "I couldn't stand the thought of them pitying me. It was already so embarrassing, being dumped by the woman I thought I was going to spend my life with.

Lying about it seemed way easier at the time." It still did.

"Oh, Soph. Your mom must've been so mad at you." The compassion in Gina's tone caught Sophia off guard, as if Gina truly understood how hard it had been to pull off that lie. Considering how close they'd once been, perhaps she did. The only thing Gina wouldn't be able to comprehend was the deeper motivation behind the omission. Even Sophia didn't really understand why she'd allowed her family to blame her for the breakup for so long instead of revealing the truth.

"Never mind. It's been years." Sophia looped her arm around Gina's, giving her a tug. "Come on. Let's get this over with."

Sophia's hunch had been right about her parents' house. Like the town of Sholan Falls, it hadn't changed one bit. The same furnishings were placed exactly where they'd been a decade previously. The familiar smell of home cooking filled the air. And the indistinguishable loudness of having all the Rossis under one roof caused the walls to vibrate. Actually, Sophia thought it might even have gotten louder. How was that possible?

As soon as they rounded the corner into the kitchen that was somehow spacious and cozy at the same time, Sophia's older sister, Bella, squealed.

"Oh my God! It's true." Ignoring Sophia completely, Bella pulled Gina into a hug made awkward by her prominent baby bump. "I thought Mom was having a menopausal fit when she said you two were back together."

Gina's eyes fell to the protrusion, a shell-shocked expression on her face. "Are you…?"

Too late, Sophia realized she'd overlooked the important step of bringing Gina up-to-date on the Rossi family. If her kin were going to believe they were back together, Sophia was going to have to cover for her mistake, quick. "Don't you remember, Gina? I told you about Bella's baby right after I mentioned Carrie was getting married this summer."

"What? Oh, that's right." Gina nodded in an exaggerated way, showing that she'd caught on. "I guess I didn't realize how close her due date was."

"I'm seven months in, and let me tell you, I'm ready to get this tiny human out of me." Bella caressed her baby bump lovingly. "I'm surprised Soph thought to mention it. She's around so little I wasn't convinced she'd remember."

"That's not true," Sophia protested, although technically, it had been well over a year since her last visit, an eternity by her family's standards. "I even brought a present with me for your baby shower this weekend."

"You're coming to the shower, right?" Bella demanded of Gina as Sophia stifled a groan. This invitation added an unwelcome layer of complication to their *quid pro quo* arrangement. If Gina didn't come, her family would never believe they were dating. But to get her ex to agree, Sophia could only imagine what sorts of concessions she'd be forced to make.

Luckily, her baby sister, Carrie, arrived at exactly the right moment, garnering everyone's attention the minute she walked through the door with a box of freshly printed wedding invitations, making it unnecessary for Gina to offer an answer about the baby shower. Sophia prayed by the time dinner was over, the whole thing would be long forgotten. Worst case, Sophia could tell them Gina had gotten sick. Or died. Either option worked for her.

"No way!" Setting down the box of programs, Carrie ran across the room and threw her arms around Gina. "I didn't think it was possible."

Sophia made a mental note that killing off her ex, even for pretend, wouldn't fly in the Rossi family. They'd insist on hosting the wake. It wasn't like Sophia needed to be the center of attention in her own family. Actually, that was a good thing, because despite people thinking actors always had to be the star of the show, as a middle child, she'd never been able to compete. She was used to it, but the way everyone was acting like Gina was the second coming or something kind of initiated her middle child insecurity more than Sophia cared to admit.

"There's my girl!" Sophia's dad barreled down the hallway toward them, and for a split second, Sophia considered stepping out of the way so as not to obstruct his pathway to Gina. But to Sophia's surprise, the hug was meant for her, and as she burrowed her face into his thick flannel shirt that smelled faintly of bay rum aftershave, the sharp edge of her mood softened. "Who is this?"

"Dad." Sophia rolled her eyes. "You remember Gina."

"From college?" He eyed Gina like she was a faded photograph, the uncertainty in his tone giving Sophia pause. Her father was turning sixty-four later that year, and for the first time, it struck Sophia that he wasn't a young man anymore.

"Oh, he's pulling your leg," Sophia's mom said with a laugh, helping to dispel the worst of Sophia's fear. "Of course, he remembers."

A lingering cloudiness in her father's eyes suggested otherwise, but he quickly affixed his smile. Sophia recognized it as his go-to look for avoiding a fight with his wife. How many times had he used that defensive tactic over the years?

"Anyone home?" A man called out from the entryway.

"In the kitchen, Tom," Carrie called.

In walked a short man who was a dead ringer for the type her sisters had always dated since high school. The resemblance was so pronounced, Gina's head swiveled instantly, searching out Sophia to exchange the type of bemused look that made all the good memories from their years together come flooding back.

Sophia was the only one of the three Rossi girls who'd strayed from dating the compact, dark-haired guys who were plentiful in their heavily Italian-American part of town. It was their preference, but not an expectation. Sophia smiled as she recalled the warm welcome they'd all given Gina. For as much pressure as her mother put on her not to be single, no one in her family had ever tried to tell her who she should love. Only that she should love *someone*. And marry them. And have kids, preferably after leaving Los Angeles behind for good in favor of buying a nice two-story colonial in Sholan Falls.

"Everyone sit down," Sophia's mother coaxed, ushering the family into the dining room, where a bowl of spaghetti had already been placed, along with homemade sauce, meatballs, freshly baked bread, and salad. The table was set for seven since Bella's husband, a nurse, was working a night shift at the hospital. But based on the amount of food her mother had cooked, Sophia briefly wondered whether another twenty people planned to stop by later on.

"Gina, tell us what you've been up to," Sophia's mom directed.

"Not too much to tell, really." Gina twirled her fork, the noodles going every which way. "I've been teaching at Comstock College, and I'm up for a tenure review soon. Otherwise, I've been working with Dr.

Harlowe on a documentary about the Queer movement that we plan to finish and submit to the Sundance film festival this fall. We'll be showing a snippet at the Pride Festival in May." Gina said this part to Sophia.

"Impressive," Bella said. "We always knew you'd do important work. Isn't that right, Soph?"

Sophia pushed her fork into a meatball but didn't lift it to her mouth. Her appetite had evaporated the second her sister had said the word *important*. That was exactly how Gina had described her work ten years ago when she'd told Sophia her films were too *important* to be distracted by their relationship.

Also, didn't tenure take a while? Sophia wondered exactly how long it had been since Gina left New York.

"Sophia?" It was her mom who said her name, making Sophia realize she'd fallen into a murky pool of rumination without ever answering her sister's question.

"Sorry. Long day at work." Sophia forced herself to lift the fork to her mouth and take a small bite. The food was delicious, but it did little to mask the bitter taste left behind when her family continued peppering her ex with questions without so much as asking her how her first day on the set had been.

But what did Sophia expect? A Christmas movie was hardly *important*. For a few moments, earlier in the evening, Sophia had allowed herself to sink into the false comfort and familiarity of being home again with

Gina. To let herself imagine this little charade they had going might have a glimmer of reality to it. She wouldn't let it happen again. Gina Mitchells had achieved exactly the level of greatness she'd set out to reach when she'd left Sophia behind in the dust.

And Sophia? At the end of the day, she was starring in a made-for-streaming holiday film, and not even a very good one. The cast's table read of the script that day had made that much clear. There was no substance to it. Despite the significant resources IBC was investing and the financial rewards Sophia hoped to reap as a result, it was hardly what anyone would call *important*. Especially not Gina.

Somehow, Sophia made it most of the way through dinner, choking down enough of her food to avoid her mother's sharp eye. When they'd reached the lull before dessert, Sophia's phone vibrated. She didn't dare pull it out of her pocket. Her mother wasn't the type who saw the need to be on a phone when family was around. But it kept buzzing, and everyone in the room was giving her a look that screamed *Aren't you going to answer that?*

"Excuse me a minute," Sophia said, rising from her chair and heading toward the bathroom for some semblance of privacy.

Her heart leaped to her throat when the flurry of texts from her publicist appeared on the home screen, along with a link to a Twitter post from the official Comstock College Pride Festival account, announcing Sophia Rossi as this year's grand marshal.

"Shit!" Sophia reached for the porcelain sink to support her weight. Her producer would be furious, especially being blindsided like this before she'd had a chance to smooth things over in just the right way. And if IBC was anything like the Keynote Channel had been, they would see this as an attack and want someone's head on a platter. Probably hers. She'd be fired for sure.

How could Gina have done this to me?

She should have expected it, though. Gina had proven ten years ago that she would always put her own career first. But to be betrayed right at the moment she'd started to feel that spark stirring between them again—it was just too much.

Marching into the family room, Sophia offered what she knew was the same smile her father utilized in similar situations. Gina's sober expression said she remembered it well. "I have to be on the set early tomorrow. Gina, you ready?"

"You can't go yet!" her mother wailed. "What about dessert?"

"Let it go, Angie," her father said, coming to her rescue. Maybe he'd recognized the meaning behind Sophia's stiff smile, too.

"Sophia's right." Gina released a yawn Sophia was fairly certain was less than genuine. "I have a stack of term papers that aren't going to grade themselves."

"I hope you don't have to stay up too late," Sophia's mom said with sincerity. "You must take home some cannoli." She shot out of the room, returning comically fast with a box large enough to hold at least a dozen of the promised pastries. The only thing that kept her from looking like a scene out of a Roadrunner cartoon was the lack of smoke billowing from her heels. "There's more where that came from."

Sophia made for the door before her mom could follow through with a second container. Outside, when out of view of any of the windows, Sophia allowed her face to drop its mask. Her jaw clenched as she held up her phone to Gina. "Explain this."

"What?" For her part, Gina seemed genuinely perplexed as she took the phone, her expression doing such a good job of morphing into one of horror as she took it all in that Sophia wondered if the filmmaker had ever considered working on the other side of the camera. "I'm going to kill them."

"Don't bother pretending," Sophia growled. "It wouldn't be the first time you backed me into a corner to get what you wanted. Why didn't you trust me? I just needed a day or two to go through the proper channels before you guys started pasting my image all over your social media accounts."

"That's not—okay, I see why you think I'd be capable of it. Trust me; I had no part in this, but I do plan on getting to the bottom of it."

"You do that!" Sophia stared daggers at Gina. "Meanwhile, I'll try to convince Holden Dix not to fire me."

"Who is Holden Dix?" Despite the gravity of the situation, Gina's lips twitched. Understandable, considering Sophia's producer had been given a name a porn star would envy.

"He's the one who decides if I still have a job, and if I ever get to work in Hollywood again." Sophia refused to lighten the mood by indulging in one of the hundreds of dick jokes the man's name so aptly inspired. Instead, she glared intently until the last trace of levity washed away, and her eyes shifted to the ground.

A moment later, Gina took out her own phone, tapping on the screen in a frenzy. "The tweet's gone."

Sophia crossed her arms. "The damage has been done."

Gina sighed with such anguish, Sophia almost believed she'd had as little to do with this fiasco as she claimed. "What can I do to make this up to you?"

Sophia wanted to tell her to go to hell, to leave and never speak to her again. After all, Sophia had finally gotten used to living without her ex, and she'd been doing just fine.

Instead, she said, "For starters, you're coming to my sister's baby shower with me this weekend. Don't even think about making an excuse."

Sophia felt as surprised by this turn of events as

Gina looked, but somewhat uplifted, too. Making Gina do her bidding for the next several weeks would be much more entertaining than cutting her off. Assuming Sophia could work some magic and keep from getting fired, that was.

Time to make some calls.

CHAPTER FIVE

"Just tell her what you told me," Gina urged as she and Megan approached the security guard who was standing beside the temporary barrier that had been erected to close off the film set from the rest of downtown Sholan Falls. Gina adopted her most reassuring tone as she tried to coax Megan from their hiding place behind her back.

"I don't like it when people hate me." Megan's lower lip trembled. Gina wanted to scream at them not to start crying again, but quickly thought better of it. For one thing, screaming rarely led to less crying. And considering Sophia was as softhearted as they came, tears could help their case.

"It's going to be okay," Gina soothed, hoping she was right. That Sophia had agreed to let them visit the set today after last night's fiasco was a promising sign, almost as good as knowing that at least for the moment, Sophia still had her job. Although, security was tighter today as if fearful a band of rainbow warriors would whisk away their precious Queen of Christmas.

Gina gave their names to the security guard, who spoke into a walkie-talkie to an unseen third party. An answer crackled through the device, which Gina couldn't make out but assumed must've been some form of approval, because the guard nodded, moving aside to let them through.

There was even more activity on set this morning than there had been the day before. The knot in Gina's stomach, which had been growing since leaving the Rossis' house, tightened. Though no stranger to film making, this production was like nothing she'd ever experienced. The size of the crew and the sheer amount of equipment was overwhelming, like taking one of her documentaries and force-feeding it steroids.

The much-needed reminder of how different her world and Sophia's had become was a punch to the gut, nonetheless. For a moment at dinner, before things had gone sideways with the discovery of the ill-timed tweet, Gina had felt the old spark between her and Sophia rekindling. She'd longed to bask in the warm glow of it and wasn't so naive as to think she wouldn't have been tempted to stoke the flames, too. But they didn't belong together any more now than they had ten years ago. It was best Gina remember that and focus on the task at hand—remaining on speaking terms with her ex until after the Pride Festival—rather than indulging in pointless fantasies.

Exiting one of the trailers that had been set up alongside the town common, Sophia made her way over. Megan let out a terrified yelp before ducking behind Gina again. Sophia slowed as she got closer, giving Gina a questioning look before saying, "Good morning."

"Hi," Gina said, wishing Megan would stop impersonating a shadow long enough to smooth things over rather than leaving it all to her. "I found out what happened with the tweet. It was a huge mistake."

"Huge," echoed Megan, still not coming into view.

"Yes, I think we'd already established that." Not a trace of the earlier warmth could be found in Sophia's eyes. Even though Gina knew she shouldn't let that bother her, it stung.

"It's your bloody American dates," Megan declared, finding some bravery after all.

"Excuse me?" Sophia's features settled into a scowl.

Gina sighed, fearing Megan's input had done more harm than good to Sophia's mood. "Megan here was designing some graphics for the festival's social media pages. When they went to schedule the posts, they meant to choose May fourth but selected April fifth instead."

"I… I'm so sorry," Megan stammered. "If I got you in trouble, I'll just die."

"Please, don't do that." Sophia offered the young student an encouraging smile. She'd always been kind, and it lifted Gina's heart to see the years hadn't changed that. "As it happens, my publicist was able to smooth things out with the network higher-ups."

"That's great," Gina began. "How did—?"

"What the fuck, Sophia?" a man barked, charging at them with all the grace of an angry bull. Gina's hackles went up instantly. "Time is money. Don't you have a scene to be running instead of standing around gabbing?"

"It's hard to start rehearsals when my co-star hasn't shown up yet, Mr. Dix," Sophia answered.

This was the infamous Holden Dix? Gina choked back a laugh. The balding man certainly lived up to his name.

"What are you talking about?" the producer demanded. "Where the hell is Butch? And who are they?" The man jerked his head to Gina and Megan. "If they're extras, did they get the memo that this is a Christmas flick? They look like hobos."

"These are two of the people from the Comstock College Pride Festival I was telling you about earlier," Sophia explained in an even tone that Gina knew from experience meant she was holding in her wrath.

"She's not going to be in your little festival." Mr. Dix eyed Gina and Megan with the type of look usually reserved for gum—or something worse—that had gotten stuck to the bottom of a shoe. It was a look

Gina had experienced from a Hollywood producer before, her senior year of college when she'd been told a Black lesbian would never be able to write a romantic comedy that would sell. This man's unmerited scorn brought all the pain of that rejection back in a rush, shaking Gina from the inside out with impotent rage.

"Mr. Dix," Sophia argued, but he held up a hand, silencing her.

"You heard me. What's next on the *kick some ass* list?" The man greedily rubbed his hands together, clearly relishing his tough guy street cred. Or was it simply bluster due to his bald head that made him a walking caricature of his last name? Had neither of his parents said the name aloud to see what a name like that would saddle a person with their whole life?

"I don't think you understand," Sophia persisted, earning new respect from Gina, who wished she'd found similar courage ten years ago when faced with a similarly arrogant ass. "My publicist worked it out with the company last night."

"As the producer of this film, I *am* the company." The man's face had grown red, and spittle flew from his mouth as he took a step closer to Sophia.

Instinctively, Gina inched closer, angling her body to be able to step between them if the situation called for it. She may have been meek when she was in college, but life had taught her a thing or two since then, and she refused to allow anyone to bully Sophia.

Perhaps sensing this, the man took a step back, leveling a finger at Sophia as he added, "Don't you dare go over my head."

"I would never." Sophia placed a hand over her heart in an award-worthy act of innocence that Gina knew was total bullshit. It was a good thing the woman wasn't looking in her direction because Gina wasn't sure she'd be able to stop herself from grinning and putting her hand up for a high five. "In fact, even *I* wasn't informed until just a few minutes ago. Mr. Abrams's assistant called to let me know my participation in the festival was a go. I'm sure you're next on the list."

As if on cue, the man's phone rang. Tight-lipped, he stepped out of earshot to take the call.

"Who is that beast?" Megan asked, finally finding their voice. "Is he always like that?"

"Believe it or not, that is the man known in the industry as Mr. Christmas," Sophia said, gritting her teeth. "He's not usually that nice."

"Are you positive he'll let you be our grand marshal?" Gina asked, guilt pooling in her belly for having dragged Sophia into this mess.

"He won't be given a choice. My publicist managed to explain to his boss's boss just how badly IBC could use some points with the LGBTQ+ community."

"Why is that?" Gina asked.

"They've been raked over the coals for killing off a popular lesbian character on one of their shows."

Sophia's eyes held a glint of mischief that suggested she'd been the one to come up with that particular line of attack. "Despite the good press the news division has enjoyed from having Dakota Washington and Amanda Morgan on the team, the entertainment side is taking a beating. My publicist simply reminded them of this fact."

"That's all it took?" Gina waited for the other shoe to drop.

"Not exactly." Sophia's eyes fluttered shut. "There were a few concessions I had to agree to for the duration of my current contract."

"Concessions?" Gina had a sinking feeling. Whatever Sophia had been strong-armed into, it didn't sound good. "What kind of concessions?"

"While the company is aware that I identify as bisexual and is willing to allow me to participate in the festival, they've requested that I do not engage in any behavior that could be construed as... well, that is to say—"

"They're forbidding you from doing anything gay?" Megan interjected, clearly incensed. "That's unconstitutional. You could sue!"

"I would lose," Sophia told the student gently, giving voice to exactly the thought that was in Gina's head. "They were subtler in their wording, and I got the impression it was mostly a move to make sure they could get Holden Dix onboard with the decision."

"That's bullshit," Megan argued. "That man can't

dictate—wait, is your producer's name really Holden Dix?"

"Some things you simply can't make up," Sophia confirmed.

Gina chuckled as she glanced at the producer, who was red-faced and screaming into his phone like a spoiled child having a tantrum.

"Even though no one else goes by their last name on set, everyone always calls him Mr. Dix," Sophia said. "He thinks it's a sign of respect."

"He's that dumb?" Megan asked.

"Most men in his position are," Sophia said. "He's scared. His last two movies at Keynote came in past deadline and over budget, only to get panned. Lucky for him, he'd already signed the contract with IBC, but my gut says if this one doesn't go right, he'll be out on his bum here just like he would've been at Keynote if he hadn't quit in the St. Nick of time."

"Couldn't happen to a nicer Dix." Megan paused before saying, "I *am* really sorry. I didn't mean to get you into trouble. Not after you saved our asses."

"It's okay," Sophia told Megan with a sincerity that despite her fine acting skills, Gina believed to be completely genuine.

"But now you're in trouble, and you've had to agree to a completely terrible arrangement." Megan pointed to Mr. Dix, who had ended his phone call and was now railing at some hapless woman who'd been passing by. "Does he hate women?"

Sophia blew out a breath. "I think it's safe to say he hates everyone."

"Why do jerks like that always seem to stay in control?" Megan asked as Mr. Dix kicked the gazebo. He immediately seemed to regret it, hopping on one foot and screaming obscenities. "Anyway, Ms. Rossi, everyone at the college really appreciates what you're doing for us."

"Call me Sophia, and it's my pleasure." A hint of something troubling passed over her face but disappeared before Gina could figure out what it was. "Unfortunately, misogyny still rules Hollywood. They're just getting better at sugar coating it."

"We really should get going," Gina said, directing the comment at Megan. "We've taken up enough of Sophia's time. She has a full day of rehearsals and fittings ahead of her."

"Yeah, and my morning class starts in thirty minutes," Megan added. "I can't believe it's after ten already."

"Is it?" Sophia glanced at her phone, frowning. "Where is Butch? He was supposed to be here over an hour ago."

"Is he usually late?" Gina asked.

Sophia frowned. "No, and we've worked together a number of times."

"Will Mr. Dix speak to Butch the way he did to you?"

"Not a chance. Butch is one of Dix's favorite leading men."

"Handsome and dumb as bricks?" Gina guessed, earning her a laugh from both Sophia and Megan.

"Sophia!" The production assistant Gina had met the day before came running up, winded and looking like he'd been chased across the common by Satan himself. "I just got a call from the local hospital. Butch was in a motorcycle accident this morning. I don't have details, but it sounded bad."

"Oh, God!" Sophia gasped, teetering in a way that made Gina fear she would pass out.

Without pausing to think, Gina rushed to steady her, wrapping an arm around Sophia's waist. At the same time, she turned to toss her car keys to Megan. "Why don't you take my car, and head back to campus so you don't miss class? I'm going to stay here to make sure Sophia's okay."

CHAPTER SIX

"They say he's got a broken collar bone and abrasions all along his left side." Sophia settled beside Gina on a bench near the gazebo, the scent of fresh paint and sawdust thick in the air.

"What does that mean for today? And for after, I guess?" The concern in Gina's tone warmed places inside Sophia she'd barely known were there, and it took all her willpower not to curl herself into a ball against her ex's soft, welcoming body.

"They've told us to go home and report back tomorrow at our regular call times," Sophia answered, exhaustion clouding her brain as she tried to work through all the possible long-term scenarios at once. "They'll have to replace him. I don't see how Butch would heal fast enough to work, considering we're supposed to film this whole thing in six weeks."

"Six?"

Sophia laughed as Gina's eyebrows shot halfway up her forehead. "That's a luxury. I'm used to filming in three."

Gina's jaw went slack. "How do you film an entire movie in three weeks?"

"With extreme efficiency," Sophia replied. "Keynote has mastered the art of it, which is how they can make thirty new Christmas films in a year. This is IBC's first, and they're willing to part with the resources for a higher production value, within reason. Time is still money, which means they'll have to start recasting right away."

"They won't consider a delay?"

"For an actor?" Sophia let out a grunting laugh. "Heck no. We have a crew of twenty-five people getting paid by the day, plus the cost of equipment and permits. Do you have any idea what the pitch to delivery cycle was supposed to be on this project? Four months."

"From concept to finished product?" Gina let out a low whistle. "I don't see how that's even possible. I wouldn't have thought a network like IBC ran on those kind of time constraints."

"I don't think they do, normally," Sophia answered, grateful for a few minutes of mundane shop talk to clear her head. "But since the Christmas market is a new one for them, they brought in Dix as an expert.

He learned everything he knew working at Keynote, so that's how we're doing it here, too."

"What are you going to do now?" Gina asked.

"You mean this very second?" Sophia shrugged. "Go back to my room at the inn, I guess. Hide there and hope my mom doesn't hear I got the day off."

"But, it's a beautiful spring day. Staying inside on a day like this should be illegal."

"I see that part of your personality hasn't changed." Sophia gave Gina a nudge with her shoulder. "The whole carpe diem thing."

"You used to like that about me…" Gina let her voice trail off, as if recalling all the reasons she'd given Sophia not to like her anymore.

Instead of dwelling on it, Sophia laughed. The more time she spent around her ex, the more she realized how much water had flowed under that bridge, enough that carrying a grudge was hardly worth the effort and exhaustion. "I still can't wrap my brain around this whole bizarre situation."

"What part of it?" Gina asked.

"Us pretending we're dating when around my family, for one thing. And now having to hide the fact we're pretending to date, thanks to my homophobic producer."

"I've never met a more aptly named man," Gina commented dryly. "But you're right, it could be a plot from a terrible made-for-TV movie."

"I don't know." Sophia paused, questioning whether to reveal the rest of her thought. Up until now, she'd kept her opinions close to the vest, but this was Gina. She'd understand. "Even that sounds better than this third-rate script I'm working with."

Gina tilted her head. "I thought you were excited by this project."

"I am," Sophia rushed to clarify. "Don't get me wrong. The opportunity is amazing. If this project goes well, I'm looking at a multi-film contract, even producer credits and a twenty-percent cut of international rights down the road. But remember that Christmas movie drinking game we played in college?"

"Only very vaguely," Gina said with a laugh. "Which I assume means I played it correctly."

"It was when you were working on your script, back when you were still writing rom-coms instead of changing the world." *Back when we shared the same dreams.* Sophia pressed her lips together tightly as she tried to squeeze the bitterness from her tone, which crept in whenever she thought of that happy time before her world had come crashing down. "We made a list of all the corny tropes and plot devices we could think of before the Christmas countdown started. Then we took shots every time one showed up."

"I do remember that." Gina cleared her throat, and Sophia could almost imagine she was trying to clear away the emotion lodged there. Or maybe it was only

Sophia who still got choked up reminiscing about those days. "How drunk would we get from your current script?"

"Blackout level," Sophia assured her. "Like go on a two-week bender and wake up with a stranger's name tattooed across your ass kind of drunk."

Gina's face lit up, and she rubbed her hands together in obvious glee. Picking apart terrible movies had been one of their favorite hobbies in college. "Tell me more."

"This is a classic," Sophia said. "Successful girl leaves the big city to come home and help run the family business after her father has a stroke."

"Let me guess. The family business is a Christmas tree farm."

"Nope. Strike one." Sophia acted out being a home plate umpire. "Try again."

"What happens if I strike out?"

"You don't get to spend the day with me."

"That's not fair!"

"Why not?" Sophia's heart fluttered as Gina looked away, visibly flustered.

"It's a commonly known fact these movies have twenty-four plot variations, and I only have two guesses left. There's a lot riding on this."

"Twenty-four plot points?" Sophia asked as casually as she could to hide how her heart had clenched to discover that Gina actually wanted to spend the day together. She'd tossed out the consequences willy-nilly, only to realize as soon as they were out of her mouth how desperately she wanted Gina to stick around.

Just for the day, of course. Nothing more than that.

"Yes. It's very scientific, being the exact number needed to fill out a BINGO card."

"I'll have to trust you on that," Sophia teased. "You're the professor, and I've always hated math."

"Do I get any clues?"

"No way." Sophia enjoyed seeing the panic in Gina's eyes.

"Fine," Gina practically growled. "I'm ruling out the royalty angle right now, given the location."

"Unless my character doesn't know she's a princess." Sophia arched a brow in the way she recalled used to drive Gina crazy.

"Mind games? Really?" From the way Gina shifted her body, Sophia suspected her eyebrow trick still had the desired effect.

That was useful to know.

On the other side of the common, Sophia heard her producer let loose a steady stream of profanity. She hopped to her feet, reaching out to give Gina a hand up. "Let's get out of here."

"Worried chatting with your ex will violate your *don't act gay* clause?" Gina razzed, following Sophia.

"More like I'm afraid he'll spot me and decide to kill off my character out of spite."

"Oh, I know enough about these movies to know *that* will never happen." Gina's tone took on a sharp edge as she added, "That's why they don't like to have gay characters or minorities. You're not allowed to kill anyone off in a Christmas movie."

Sophia led the way down a side street, past the local hamburger joint that, according to the sign, had been sitting on the same corner for sixty-seven years,

"Do you remember puking in the parking lot over there?" Sophia asked, recalling the first holiday break Gina had spent with her in Sholan Falls during college.

"It's the reason I still hate pickles."

"It *wasn't* the pickles," Sophia scolded. "We drank way too much, which is apparently a theme from our misspent youth."

"The pickles didn't help," Gina argued, although it was clear her mood was lifting. "Not at all."

"Tequila shots are never a wise decision. Look at this." Sophia pointed to the freshly laid asphalt. "It must be the new rail trail. I think Mom said it opened last week. Boo's Burgers put in the bike rack to encourage families to stop for a bite."

"It's funny. So much has changed but not really. I mean, Boo's Burgers is still here. Your parents' house is the same. And yet…"

A weight settled in Sophia's chest. "I know. Sometimes it's like I've never been here before. Like I don't belong."

"I get that, although you've been back more

recently than I have. Until yesterday, I hadn't stepped foot in Sholan Falls since college."

"But... you live almost next door." Sophia wanted to ask Gina why she'd stayed away, if it had been because of her, but didn't think it wise. Most likely, Gina had been too busy doing important things, and it had nothing to do with Sophia at all. "Boo's Burgers are the best. When filming is done, we're going there for victory burgers."

"It's a date!"

Sophia faked a coughing attack to cover for the sudden giggle that bubbled up from her throat at that unexpected word. A date? Sure, that was what they were pretending they were doing, at least to Sophia's family. But technically, by the time filming was over, their arrangement would be, too. Did that mean their trip to Boo's Burgers would be a real date?

Don't be an idiot.

"How did you end up teaching?" Sophia asked, fishing for some way to change the conversation.

Gina groaned, which was not the reaction Sophia had expected. "You know what they say. There are those who do, and then there are those who teach."

"Nonsense." Sophia eyed Gina with disbelief. "You're a brilliant documentarian. You had a film nominated for an IDA."

"Eight years ago, and it didn't win. Look where that got me." Gina made a ta-da motion with her hand.

"Documentaries don't bring in the big bucks, so... I needed a Plan B."

"Professor isn't a bad Plan B."

"If you get tenure," Gina corrected. "And if your department head likes you."

"Didn't you say you were working with Dr. Harlowe?" From what Sophia could remember, Gina had been teacher's pet in the pretentious professor's classes in undergrad.

The silence was deafening.

"You still love making documentaries, right?" Sophia's pulse sped up as she contemplated what a waste it all would be if Gina wasn't happy after everything she'd given up. "You said it was your dream. Your calling."

It was why you left me, she all but screamed in her head.

"Sure. Of course." Gina offered one of her trademark shrugs, but it lacked her usual smugness. "Never fear. I may not make the big bucks, but I'll never quit."

"Money isn't everything," Sophia countered, "and if you think I'm rolling in the dough, you couldn't be more wrong."

"Whatever, Miss Movie Star."

Sophia's eyes narrowed. "You know what I earned on my first few films? Two grand a week. And if I didn't book another gig within a week of getting back to LA, I was making lattes at the local coffee place to pay rent."

Gina made a pshaw sound. "You seem to be doing okay now."

"Sure, after ten years," Sophia admitted, a swell of pride in her breast. "I have a cushion. I can pay the bills, put money into retirement, and live off savings for a while in between roles. But I have to be smart, and I'm no star. Not everyone has Lana Turner's luck, being discovered at a malt shop only to go on to have a successful fifty-year career."

"You don't want to be like Turner."

"Because she was also a pin-up model? Hell, she made more than me in the 1940s."

"She had a very unhappy life, for all her success," Gina answered in a sober tone that cut short any further argument. "Did you know her father was murdered? She was divorced seven times, too, and that was just the tip of the iceberg. She had professional luck, but it stopped there. You deserve success *and* happiness."

"In this business, it seems like you either get one or the other, but not both."

Gina stopped in her tracks, staring deeply into Sophia's eyes. "Don't ever doubt you can have both. I know you. You're a fighter who doesn't settle. Don't you dare start now."

Sophia fell silent and continued walking, turning her focus to the movement of her feet on the dark asphalt path. A fighter who didn't settle? It didn't sound like her, whatever Gina might think. If either of those things had been true, she never would have agreed to let Gina dump her without putting up more of a fight. Because it was becoming increasingly clear, the more time she and Gina spent together, that if anyone could bring her happiness in this life, it was her ex.

If only it wasn't ten years too late to fight for her.

CHAPTER SEVEN

"Who's ready to smell some dirty diapers?" Gina stood outside the brightly painted Victorian bed and breakfast where Sophia was staying. They'd agreed to meet on Saturday morning so they could show up to the Rossi house together like an official couple.

"What are you talking about?" Sophia stepped onto the porch wearing a floral dress that ended right above the knee. It was exactly the right outfit for the occasion, modest yet stylish, and Gina found she couldn't tear her eyes away from the woman's shapely, tanned calves. The sudden stirring of attraction would help her sell the authenticity of their relationship to Sophia's family today, but Gina feared she might start believing it herself.

"I've never been to a baby shower before, so I did some research," Gina explained, dragging her eyes upward to Sophia's face. "By that, I mean I fell into a YouTube rabbit hole. Apparently, there are a lot of games."

"You didn't know that?" Sophia wore a bemused expression that said Gina's ignorance on such matters was more adorable than surprising.

"If I'd known that, do you think I would've agreed to attend without putting up more of a fight? I already had to dig out my nice clothes on a day I would usually wear sweats." Gina gestured to the crisp trousers and silk blouse she'd chosen, secretly pleased when Sophia's gaze lingered on the low-cut neckline.

Not that she'd chosen it for that reason.

"Too late to back out now," Sophia warned.

"But, Soph," Gina argued. "One of the most popular games involves dumping baby food into a diaper, and you have to guess the food. That's gross."

"We're definitely playing it. My aunts love that game." It was clear Sophia enjoyed watching Gina squirm.

"I'm not backing out," Gina said as she headed toward her parked car, "but I want to put this out there. Our Christmas movie BINGO game is far better."

"Agreed." Sophia pointed to Gina's car. "Oh, good. You got it back from your student in one piece."

"Yes, but my stash of granola bars in the driver's side door was sadly depleted." Gina opened the passenger door for Sophia, stepping aside to allow her to get in. "I think Megan was stress eating after the encounter with you."

"Don't worry. You won't need them today." Sophia set the two gift bags she'd been carrying on the floor and buckled her seatbelt. "You know how my mom is about food. And, there's going to be cake."

"Let's hope it isn't baby-shaped because I'm not sure I can cut into a baby." Despite her words, Gina chuckled to herself. Ever since seeing Sophia again after so long, Gina had this feeling of elation that was hard to tamp down, let alone control.

"Was that something else you saw on the internet?" Sophia asked when Gina sat down behind the wheel. "It sounds like you found a real horror show down that rabbit hole."

"You have no idea," Gina confirmed. "There's not going to be a gender reveal, is there? One with fireworks? They don't go well, from everything I've found. Given the troubles you're already having on the set, I don't think it's wise for you to be anywhere near an exploding cannon or something."

"Knowing Bella, she's absolutely opposed to the idea. I doubt she's even asked the baby's gender, as she's always explaining how it's nothing but an outdated social construct. Sometimes, I think my sisters are more LGBTQ+ than I am." Sophia sighed. "I'm really hoping she likes my—er, *our* gifts."

"What did you—uh, *we*—get her?" Gina craned her neck as she slipped the key into the ignition, trying to catch a peek, but Sophia pulled the bags shut. "Why didn't you ask me to go shopping with you?"

"It didn't even cross my mind."

"Oh." Well, that pretty much stamped out Gina's happy feeling. Apparently, as far as Sophia was concerned, it was out of sight, out of mind.

Perhaps sensing she'd said the wrong thing, Sophia quickly added, "I bought something before I came back to town, and Mom didn't trust me to have chosen correctly, so she dropped off another gift yesterday. I'll give my sister the gift my mom bought, and you can give her what I originally intended to."

"What is it?" Gina asked with growing alarm. "It's something awful, isn't it? Probably frilly and pink. Is this your way of making sure your sister hates me?"

"Are you kidding?" Sophia scoffed. "I would have thought it was clear after dinner the other night that my sister is way more excited to have you at the shower today than me. But just to soothe your nerves, it's a pack of onesies in appropriately gender-neutral colors."

"Thank goodness."

"You know if I let you show up with a terrible gift, my family would blame me for sabotaging you. As if I wasn't already the black sheep of the family for moving out west. I don't need another mark against me, considering they'll definitely disown me when I eventually have to break the news we've broken up again."

Despite an immediate stab in the gut at the reminder of how temporary their newfound connection was, Gina forced a laugh. "Do you think your mom is buying our story?"

"I mean..." Sophia hesitated. "I think she wants to, but she isn't dumb. Be on the lookout for tests today."

"Just what I need," Gina said with a groan.

She turned onto Sophia's parents' street and could see the Rossi house from half a block away. The front yard was covered in all things baby, though as Sophia had predicted, the balloons had a gender-neutral yellow and green color scheme.

There was already an excited buzz inside the house as they entered, and Gina instantly identified dozens of familiar faces. Apparently, every single friend and family member had managed to stay on good terms over the past ten years, making Gina the only odd one out. And yet, the minute she'd walked through the door, she was enveloped in hugs and had her cheeks kissed more times than she had in all the intervening years combined. As an only child whose parents had not kept in close touch with their extended families, it was completely overwhelming.

But also kind of nice.

"Time for the games!" Mrs. Rossi announced brightly before Gina had a moment to catch her breath. "It's such a nice spring day, so I set everything up out back."

Sophia shot Gina an apologetic look as they followed the rest of the guests into the backyard.

The space was even more decorated than the front, with dozens of lawn chairs set up beneath a big popup tent to accommodate the crowd. As soon as Gina and Sophia had taken seats, Mrs. Rossi dragged Bella to the center of the tent. Sophia's other sister, Carrie, walked around the circle, handing everyone a spool of ribbon and a small pair of craft scissors. Gina tried to recall a game that began like this from the videos she'd watched but was baffled.

"Okay, ladies," Mrs. Rossi said in a booming voice. "The goal of this game is to guess how much ribbon it will take to fit around Bella's baby belly. You have one minute, and no touching or trying to measure."

While the others laughed, Gina was horrified. If there ever was a social pitfall guaranteed to put her on the outs with Sophia's sister for good, this had to be it.

"Is she serious?" Gina whispered to Sophia.

"I think so." Sophia was already dutifully unspooling her ribbon, a determined look on her face.

As the rest of the guests began to do the same, Gina eyed their results, hoping for a clue of how to proceed. Mrs. Rossi seemed determined to use as much ribbon as possible, so at least Gina wasn't likely to embarrass herself by having the most insultingly long piece.

"Mother!" Bella hollered when she caught what her mother was doing. "How large do you think I am?"

"Oh, don't be so sensitive. It's just a game." Mrs. Rossi waved a dismissive hand. "Five seconds left!"

Looking at her own spool, Gina cut a piece about half the length of Mrs. Rossi's, just as the timer began to buzz.

"Close call," Sophia teased.

"I forgot how stress-inducing your family could be."

Stress-inducing, yes, but also fun. When it was Gina's turn to test her ribbon, somehow, she was only off by an inch.

"We have a winner!" Mrs. Rossi declared.

"This is why you're my favorite sister," Bella said, not seeming to understand the meaning of her words.

Sophia arched a *you see* eyebrow, but Gina couldn't help noticing the giddy feeling spreading throughout her body, only to be doused by a wave of regret. This was all temporary. If things had been different, she might have belonged here for real, but Gina's choices ten years ago had made that impossible.

What else could she have done? When they'd both planned to move to LA, Gina as a screenwriter and Sophia as an actor, their future together had made sense. But when it had been impressed upon Gina by a real Hollywood producer that she would never make it as a screenwriter—not that she'd ever shared that tidbit with anyone, including Sophia—everything had changed. Sophia had declared she would follow Gina anywhere, including to New York where Gina had a few connections via Dr. Harlowe in documentary films.

They might have been happy for a year or two. But the New York acting scene was all wrong for Sophia, and Gina had known it. Sophia was meant for the big screen. Cobbling together enough off-Broadway shows to afford living in an apartment the size of a bread box would have wasted her talent, making her grow resentful with each passing day. Gina couldn't bear that. So she'd broken it off because somebody had to. Now Sophia was starring in exactly the types of movies she'd always loved, so surely, Gina had made the right decision.

Although, according to Sophia, it hadn't lived up to the hype. Had Hollywood been that much better for her, after all?

No. Don't do that to yourself.

Breaking up with Sophia, and not being able to tell her why, had been the hardest thing Gina had ever done. More than likely, she wouldn't be able to do it again if it were happening today. Now that she was ten years older, Gina knew how rare love was—something to be cherished. And family, too. Gina had been nothing but a disappointment to her own parents, who disapproved of her lesbian "lifestyle choice," because yes, that was what they thought it was. If she'd known then how much she was losing by letting Sophia go, she would've been more selfish about it.

"Okay. It's time for another game. This one is

called pass the water balloon." Mrs. Rossi clapped her hands together while several guests looked around with obvious confusion.

"Water balloons?" Sophia stared at her mother like the woman had forgotten to take her meds. "It's only April."

"It's warm," Mrs. Rossi said, brushing off the complaint.

"Not warm enough for water balloons," Sophia argued, though it was clear she wouldn't win.

"How is this baby-related?" Gina whispered.

"It isn't," Sophia replied, but instead of looking baffled, she was staring daggers at her mother. "She's up to something."

"Everyone, partner up. You two, over here," Mrs. Rossi insisted, nearly dragging Gina and Sophia from their chairs. "Okay. You have to pass off the water balloon to your neighbor without using your hands. Here, you two show them." Instead of demonstrating herself, Mrs. Rossi tucked a water balloon under Sophia's chin. "Now, pass it off to Gina."

"How?" It came out garbled since Sophia didn't want to move her lips too much.

"Be creative." Mrs. Rossi's eyes were filled with mischief. "It's the whole point of the game."

Realizing there would be no getting out of this until they at least gave it a try, Gina did the only thing she could think of, pressing her body against Sophia's. It was the closest they'd been to one another since the surprise kiss attack Sophia had launched on set that first day, and this time there was less shock to dull Gina's senses. Every detail of the moment was clear, like watching a movie on a high-definition screen.

Gina could smell the gardenia scent of Sophia's shampoo, hear the hitch in her breath as their breasts came together with nothing but a few thin layers of fabric between them as heat built like a bonfire. If this game lasted much longer, Gina reckoned they'd be able to roast marshmallows between them. Maybe that was part of Mrs. Rossi's plan. The woman was crazy about dessert.

Sophia widened her eyes at the contact, angling her chin to get the balloon to transfer, but it slipped, forcing Gina to reposition. Her face became practically buried in Sophia's cleavage, which wasn't helping Gina's concentration.

"Don't let it fall," Mrs. Rossi tittered, clearly pleased with herself.

Gina and Sophia contorted this way and that, their body heat switching to boiling, as they tried to accomplish the goal of getting the balloon safely tucked under Gina's chin.

Right when it seemed all was lost, they succeeded. Sophia pulled away, rolling her neck side to side, strained but beautiful.

"We should move onto the next game," Sophia's mother declared triumphantly, even though half the teams were still struggling to complete their task. "Who wants to play the memory game?"

Gina, the balloon still tucked under her chin, was more confused than she'd been all day. Considering how out of practice she was at large family gatherings, that was saying something.

Sophia plucked the balloon away, allowing Gina to stretch out her muscles. "My mother is as subtle as a marching band."

Gina stood closer to whisper in Sophia's ear, "What do you mean?"

"If I'm not mistaken," Sophia kept an eye on her mother as she spoke, "that was one of those tests I told you to be on the lookout for."

"You think she was trying to put us in a compromising situation to make us fall back in love with each other?"

"I wouldn't put it past her," Sophia confirmed. "If she thinks her little tricks are going to work, she has another thing coming."

Gina nodded in agreement, but deep down she knew that balloon game had opened her eyes, among other parts of her, to an uncomfortable truth. Little tricks or not, falling back in love with Sophia Rossi was going to be impossible for Gina to avoid. For one simple reason. Gina had never stopped loving her in the first place.

CHAPTER EIGHT

On Monday morning, Sophia woke with a start and stared at the lace canopy above her bed as a knot the size and weight of a bowling ball formed in her stomach. Grabbing her phone from the nightstand, she scanned for new messages and found none. No news was supposed to be good news, but she struggled to shake her unease. With the seriousness of Butch's injuries, would they really start filming today?

Mr. Dix had sworn on his mother's grave that was the case. "The show must go on," he'd declared. Only this wasn't some little community theater production of *Romeo and Juliet* they were trying to pull off but a feature-length film for a major production company. They had already cancelled filming so very last minute more than once, each time swearing it would only be for a day. Until the next day. Mr. Dix's assurances wore thin, and as far as Sophia was aware, Mr. Dix's mother was still alive and well, so swearing on her grave was hardly convincing and shone a spotlight on his true character. She also knew if this film fell further behind schedule and started running over budget, there would be hell to pay.

Though the sun had barely begun to send pink tendrils into the dark sky, the set was awash in activity when Sophia arrived. She reported to the wardrobe trailer for her costume, followed by hair and makeup. No one in either department had seen Butch.

"The reporter is here for that Pride Festival interview," Matt told Sophia as she exited the trailer. "She's waiting for you near the gazebo."

"Thanks." Sophia pulled her red peacoat close against the lingering chill in the air. Once again it struck her how nice it was to be filming in early spring when the weather was cooler. Pretending to be cold on a blistering July day was harder than most people gave her credit for.

"Over here!" Sophia waved enthusiastically as she spotted Gina crossing the common with her three students trailing her like ducklings. "You didn't have any trouble with security, did you?"

"No." Gina offered a hesitant smile that left Sophia wondering what had brought on the sudden shyness. Perhaps it was the looming prospect of an interview on national morning television that had Gina tongue-tied, but Sophia couldn't help thinking it had something to do with the baby shower over the weekend. Ever since the water balloon game, Gina hadn't seemed able to make eye contact without blushing.

It was kinda cute.

"Mr. Dix is clamping down more than usual," Sophia explained, feeling her own cheeks tingle over the memory of Gina's chest pressed against hers. Thank goodness her makeup was caked so thick there was little chance of any color making it through to the surface. "News of Butch's accident has paparazzi swarming to get photos, and that's the last thing Mr. Dix wants."

"Then why are we here for the television interview?" Megan asked—quite astutely, in Sophia's opinion, since the same question had occurred to her, as well. A news crew, while better than a tabloid, was still a risk if they wanted to downplay the leading man's injuries.

"The truth?" Sophia stage-whispered. "Because IBC wants more buzz and didn't clear it with Mr. Dix. If you think he's pissed about it, you have no idea."

And scared. The way IBC had disregarded the producer, whispers were everywhere that Holden Dix was on his way out. What that would mean for the rest of them, especially if Butch had to be replaced, was anyone's guess. But she'd been in the business long enough to know the worst-case scenarios, and they weren't pretty. Dix had been such a fool, claiming all Butch needed was a handful of days for a complete recovery, putting everyone at risk. It was little wonder Sophia hadn't managed much sleep.

Affixing a smile she hoped would convince everyone she hadn't a care in the world, Sophia led Gina and the students to a group of director chairs that had been set up for the interview. Both the reporter and her cameraman were already in place.

"Ms. Rossi?" The young woman held out her hand, which Sophia shook. "I'm Missy Taylor from the local IBC affiliate in Springfield."

"Please, call me Sophia. This is Gina Mitchells and —" Sophia stopped short, realizing Megan's name was the only one she could remember from the email chain.

Without missing a beat, Gina stepped in to introduce the others, who each took their seats, leaving the two chairs closest to the reporter for Sophia and Gina to occupy.

A sudden look of concentration came over Missy's face as she pressed a finger to her ear. "Showtime."

The cameraman counted down as someone in The AM Show's New York studio handed off the interview to Missy. "I'm here with Sophia Rossi, in her hometown of Sholan Falls. Sophia, what's it like filming a Christmas movie where you grew up?"

"It's a dream come true, Missy," Sophia answered,

slipping effortlessly into her public persona, a character she'd created who was similar to her real self, only without any of the awkwardness and crippling self-doubt that might otherwise plague her in front of a camera. "I've always thought my town was the perfect setting for a holiday movie, aside from the missing gazebo. But our production team has built a gorgeous one, and it'll stay put long after we're gone as our gift to the town."

Giddiness bubbled up inside Sophia as she imagined the old ladies at the historical society fuming over that. Sometimes it was the little things that brightened the day.

"How special. It's not the only way you're helping the area, though, is it? For those of you at home, you may have noticed four beautiful wo—people," Missy corrected with a quick glance at Megan. "We understand you've agreed to replace Lucas Brown as the grand marshal in Comstock College's Pride Parade. I imagine it's quite an honor to be grand marshal at your alma mater." Missy's voice went so high she'd probably have to fight off lascivious chipmunks on her way home.

"It really is." Sophia glanced in Gina's direction.

"I have a question for the planning committee." Missy's gaze swept Gina and the students. "Whose brilliant idea was it to ask Sophia Rossi to step in after that ugliness with Lucas Brown?"

"As you can imagine," Gina broke in, presumably to give a pre-approved message before one of the students could mess up, "as soon as we learned of the unfortunate things Mr. Brown had said, we immediately moved to make things right. It was a group effort deciding on Sophia, but I think the credit goes to fate. Who would've expected the Queen of Christmas to be just a few miles down the road?"

"Were you concerned she would say no, given the unfortunate event immersing the former grand marshal into hot water?" Missy pressed, her voice sounding as dramatic as if Lucas Brown had been the President of the United States caught on a hot mic instead of a comedian knowingly dunking himself into the mess, triggering social media warriors to attack.

Before Gina could answer, Megan chimed in. "We were way more worried when we found out our professor had dumped Sophia and broken her heart when they were in college. If I remember correctly, our professor said Sophia promised to hate her forever."

Looking like she'd been offered the world's juiciest steak on a silver platter, Missy took less than a second to process Megan's revelation before pouncing. "You two used to date?"

"Uh…" Sophia looked to Gina, who was doing her best to melt into her seat.

"Isn't it a small world?" Megan asked, their sudden squirming indicating the question was an attempt to redirect the conversation from their inadvertent faux pas. "The important thing is—"

"What caused the breakup?" Missy pressed, speaking over Megan.

"Gosh," Gina rubbed the back of her head, seemingly at a loss for what to say next.

Sophia started to talk, although she wasn't sure what she was going to say, and it seemed like a lifetime had passed since her mouth opened and nothing came out. Fortunately, she was spared the need to say anything when she got a gander of Butch approaching. She was instantly struck dumb. Her normally hunky costar was an utter mess.

Butch's left arm was in a sling, a foam triangle underneath it, forcing the arm to be nearly shoulder high. The left side of his face had road rash, one particular stretch looking so bad Sophia thought it would be impossible for Jane, the makeup artist, to cover it up.

As Sophia's jaw dropped, Missy swiveled around. The newscaster's reaction was even more exaggerated, though this time, Sophia didn't think the woman was putting on a show for the audience at home.

"What the—?" Megan uttered, their eyes wide. "Good God, he looks like Frankenstein's monster."

More like Dr. Jekyll—and Mr. Hyde, Sophia thought. He kind of resembled both at the same time, depending which side you were looking at.

Appearing to have forgotten Sophia, Gina, and the juicy gossip about their failed college relationship entirely, Missy motioned for the cameraman to follow her toward the battered leading man. Sophia stiffened, knowing Mr. Dix would lose it over this, but then she relaxed as she remembered that, unlike the story getting out about her college heartache, it wasn't her problem. Let the PR people deal with their mess. You didn't have to be Einstein to know things on this set wouldn't go smoothly. Not for one second.

Gina turned to Sophia. "He's not going to film like that, is he?"

"According to Mr. Dix, yes," Sophia answered, though she could hardly believe it now that she saw the man for herself. What had their producer been thinking? "Dix said we'd have to accommodate by filming Butch from one side—but, look at him. There's no way he can make it through a full film only showing one side." Sophia's face blanched.

"What about a scarf and oversized winter jacket?" Gina suggested, her expression making it clear she didn't believe her suggestion would work. "He can carry a fake poinsettia with his good arm, to block the sling. You know, like they do when someone is pregnant."

"He's live on *The AM Show* trying to act like there was nothing unusual about his appearance, and even from here, I can tell he's failing miserably." Sophia's heart sunk as she continued to watch it on the screen to the side, realizing what this meant. "There's no way the executives in LA won't hear about this."

Gina looked aghast. "They don't already know?"

"Everyone has been told to downplay it, or deny any knowledge. Hell, I didn't even know it was this bad." Sophia's voice wobbled as she fought back tears. "Now that they know the full extent of his injuries, I fear the repercussions are going to be far worse."

"They know we used to date, too," Gina added warily. "I guess that violates your *don't do anything gay* agreement, even if retroactively."

"Yeah, you think?" Sophia's stomach churned as all the bad news came crashing in at once. "Gina, I know this industry. IBC hasn't been quiet about their plan to corner the holiday movie market, and they were thrilled to get a package deal with Dix, Butch, and me coming on board all at once. But nothing has gone right. Not one dang thing."

"What do you think they'll do?" Gina's voice was low and tinged with worry as she glanced toward the news cameras. "Surely, they've invested too much money already to simply walk away."

"The sunk costs are high but nothing compared to how much it might cost if they keep going with a poorly managed production. Remember what IBC did with their news streaming channel a few months ago? They spent millions to launch that, and they pulled the plug after a month."

"You think they would do the same thing to your film?"

Sophia swallowed, her throat dry and scratchy. As

much as she hated to give voice to her fears, she couldn't lie to Gina. Not about this. "I don't know for sure, but considering the shitty script, a producer who is deceiving them, and a male lead who needs to be replaced, if I were them, I sure as heck would consider cutting my losses right now and saving face."

CHAPTER NINE

Gina got up from her kitchen table to pace her small apartment, counting each step as she went. Twenty-two steps to the teal sofa in the living room, another eight to the coatrack in the front hall. Thirty steps to make it back to the kitchen again. Despite working as diligently as she could for the past week, she still had another three papers left to grade before class the next day.

Wasting away the day was the last thing she had time for. But she couldn't stop thinking about Sophia, and the disastrous interview that morning.

No doubt the reporter from the local IBC affiliate considered it a triumph. The footage of Butch trying to run away from the cameras had been trending on Twitter all day. As far as Gina knew, the production had not been shut down, at least not yet, though it wasn't like she had any inside knowledge. But Sophia hadn't passed along any updates, and surely, she would if something bad had happened. Wouldn't she? Gina considered texting to see if there was any news, but feared it would stress Sophia out even more. Anxiety had always plagued her, and Gina didn't want to pile on.

She paced a little faster, though the increased exercise wasn't the only reason her heart started beating faster. The more time she'd spent with Sophia in the past week, the more confused and on edge Gina had become. As if Mrs. Rossi trying to get them together—literally—with the balloon game at the shower wasn't enough, now Gina had to deal with the emotional fallout from the truth about their college breakup hitting the national news.

Sophia's whole family must have seen it. Gina might have been spared their poor opinion before, thanks to Sophia's omissions of the truth, but she wouldn't be so lucky this time. Megan had as good as announced to the world what Gina had done. Of course, this new relationship of theirs wasn't real, anyway, so it shouldn't matter.

But it did.

Gina's internal battle was interrupted by a knock at the door. *Please don't be a journalist wanting the scoop on Sophia.* Gina had already turned down three requests for comment.

She peeked through the eyehole and started to laugh. *Speak of the Devil.*

"I can hear you." Sophia grinned, making her already distorted image in the little circle look even more comical.

"Are you with TMZ?" Gina pretended to sound stern. "I've already said no comment."

Gina couldn't see Sophia's eye roll, but it was palpable through the door.

"I brought Chinese, but now I'm considering eating it all myself." Sophia turned as if to leave.

"Don't you dare." Not hesitating a second longer, Gina flung the door open. "I'm starving!"

"I knew you would be, at least if you're anything like you used to be in college. You could sit in the same chair for twenty-four hours without moving until you finished whatever task you were working on." Sophia entered the apartment with a massive brown bag in her arms. The delicious smell of all things Asian teased Gina's nostrils and made her stomach gurgle in delight. "Where should I set this?"

"Is that from Wong's?" Gina practically did what she dubbed the rom-com twirl, so great was her joy over the prospect of a piping hot plate of food.

"Of course, it is," Sophia confirmed, sliding her shoulder bag off her arm and letting it rest beside the couch in the living room as she followed Gina to the kitchen. "They're the best, even after all these years."

"You can set the bag here." Gina swept up the term papers she'd been grading, transferring them from the table to a countertop to make room for them to eat. "I'll grab some plates and silverware."

"Plates, silverware, and a real table? You've gotten fancy since college." The gentle teasing in Sophia's tone set off a reaction in parts of Gina's body that had nothing to do with hunger. At least, not the kind of hunger food would address. Gina did her best to ignore it, focusing all her attention on carrying two heavy ceramic plates to the table without losing her grip.

"How were things on set after I left?" Gina asked, hoping for something to distract her from how beautiful Sophia looked with her hair swept up in a messy bun, wearing yoga pants and a hoodie.

"A total disaster." Sophia fell into one of the two chairs at Gina's tiny table, sighing. "Mr. Dix insisted we put in a full day, too."

"Poor Butch." Gina opened the bag and inhaled with satisfaction before starting to remove the containers. "Did he manage to make it through?"

"He's really trying his best, but he's on so many painkillers they're having to feed him one line at a time." Sophia reached for what turned out to be crispy orange beef, popping off the plastic lid before moving on to do the same with the next dish. From what Gina could tell, she'd ordered one of everything. "I don't know if he can last another day. He belongs in the hospital or on bedrest at the very least."

"Surely, they must at least be considering replacing

him now," Gina said, unable to hold back a smile as she heaped lo mein noodles onto her plate.

"From what I hear, Dix is scrambling to call in a favor from one of the other Keynote Channel actors he's worked with before, but I'm not sure it will matter. Rumor has it the top brass of IBC is coming out to *assess* the situation." Sophia made quote marks before using her fork to scoop some sesame chicken onto her plate.

Gina plucked an egg roll from a white, greasy bag. "Is there duck sauce?"

"Have I ever forgotten?" Sophia rummaged in the pile of condiments, tossing two packets across the table. Apparently, she also hadn't forgotten that Gina always splurged when it came to sauce.

After taking a bite, Sophia let out a satisfied moan. "It's been so long since I've had Wong's. Hands down the best Chinese on the planet."

Gina, with a mouthful of egg roll, could only nod in agreement.

"Do you get it a lot?" Sophia asked. It was an innocent enough question, but it brought the truth of their situation slamming back full force.

"Not too often." Translation: never. In all the years since Gina had returned to Comstock, she hadn't ever ordered Wong's for delivery even once. The food, like Sholan Falls, brought back too many memories.

"You have better willpower than I do." Sophia dipped a steamed dumpling into Wong's special soy and ginger sauce, seemingly oblivious to the war of emotions playing out in Gina's heart over something as simple as a meal.

Gina may have had willpower at one point in her life, but ever since Sophia had swanned back into the picture, Gina couldn't stop thinking about her ex. No matter how well intentioned she'd been, breaking up with Sophia had been the single most—*oh, shit*!

"Uh… did your mom see the interview?" Gina stared down at her pork fried rice, her appetite evaporating.

Sophia paused a beat. "Yes."

"She must hate me."

"Why?"

"Because now she knows I was the one who broke up with you."

"Oh, that." Sophia took a bite, chewing slowly, each deliberate movement of her jaw seeming to hammer another nail into their fake-relationship coffin. "Funny about that."

"Funny?" Gina had a feeling that was not the correct word.

Without looking up from her plate, Sophia said, "According to my mother, I must have done something terrible for you to dump me, because in her words, you were head over heels in love with me."

"I was." Gina refrained from clasping a hand over her mouth at this admission, not that it would've helped. The words had popped out, and there would be no putting them back in. Part of her didn't want to. The pain of why she did it clawed at her throat.

Sophia leveled her eyes at Gina, like she was searching for something—an answer, maybe? But she didn't speak, and Gina was hardly surprised. What could be said to follow that?

Finally, Sophia let out a half laugh, half snort. "Typical of my mom, though, blaming me."

"I can explain it to her if you want me to."

"Can you?" Sophia arched an eyebrow, the action having its usual effect. The question was, did Sophia do it for the old reason or out of habit?

"If it'll help," Gina mumbled, squeezing her legs together. Now was about the worst possible time to let on how turned on she was, all things considered.

"Not to my mom," Sophia said softly. "To me."

"What do you mean?" Gina was trying to buy herself a little time, but she knew exactly what Sophia wanted to hear.

"From what I remember, you wanted to go to LA as much as I did. Ever since we met our sophomore year, all you ever talked about was becoming a screenwriter. Then, right before graduation, you suddenly wanted to make documentaries instead."

"What's wrong with documentaries?" Gina leaned into her defensiveness, using it as a shield against all the painful places this conversation threatened to go.

"Nothing," Sophia insisted, her eyes glistening. "Nothing at all. What I didn't understand, and I still don't, was why you decided to move to New York City instead of LA, and why you did it alone. What happened, Gin?"

Gina's heart lurched. She'd forgotten how much she loved it when Sophia called her that. "I—"

"You were a brilliant screenwriter," Sophia pressed, emotion surging in her tone.

"No, I wasn't." Gina indulged in a low, bitter laugh. "Far from it."

"That's simply not true," Sophia argued. "I can understand if you got scared and started to doubt yourself, but why didn't you talk to me?"

"That wasn't it." Gina prayed her tone made it clear the conversation was over.

How could she explain to Sophia all these years later what had happened in the meeting with Alex Cross, a Keystone Channel producer? After all, he was the same one who had found Sophia so brilliant that her future career success had been nearly guaranteed. Yet he'd made it abundantly clear to Gina her type of stories would never sell.

So she'd given up. It had been the smart move, taking Professor Harlowe up on his offer to help break into the documentary film industry. But there'd been no way Gina could allow Sophia to throw away her chance in Hollywood by moving to New York instead.

It had been the right decision. But if that was true, why did it suddenly feel so cowardly and wrong?

"Do you still write?" Sophia asked, her voice low and subdued.

"Not in years, unless you count lectures." Gina tried laughing to lift the mood. It was less than successful. Tiring of the formality of sitting at a table, Gina grabbed one of the paper takeout containers and a pair of chopsticks and headed for the couch.

Sophia followed, looking grateful for the change. "What ever happened to that script you were working on senior year?"

"*Christmas at Rainbow Falls?* Oh gawd." Gina snorted. "I haven't thought of that in years."

Sophia settled on the couch next to Gina, not so close they were touching, but not very far, either. A single throw pillow filled the space between them, like a safety barrier. Sophia tucked her legs up under her, looking like not a day had passed since college. "Do you still have it?"

"I think so, maybe." Gina shrugged, even though she was almost certain she knew exactly where that old screenplay was, hiding in a desk drawer with all the others she hadn't been able to bring herself to get rid of.

"Can I see it?" Sophia's eyes twinkled as at least some of her good mood returned.

Gina shook her head, her curls flying. "It's atrocious. I basically wrote it on a dare, just to prove I could."

"I remember. I'm the one who dared you." Sophia's

lips twitched, a tiny dimple forming at the very edge of her mouth that melted Gina instantly. It was a dimple that could only be coaxed to appear in limited circumstances when Sophia was being particularly beguiling. Gina had nearly forgotten it existed.

"I don't know," Gina said, knowing she would give in eventually. Now that Sophia's dimple had reappeared, she would do anything to keep it from fading. Even reopen decade-old wounds.

"Humor me," Sophia pleaded. "I'm having a dreadful week."

"Oh, you still have the guilt trip down."

"Do I? Because you aren't giving in yet." Sophia batted her lashes.

"You're not playing fair." Gina uncrossed her legs and recrossed them.

"I have had a bad week, and I may be fired tomorrow, so any distraction would be welcome."

"Why don't we watch your favorite movie?" Gina offered.

"Which is?" Sophia sucked in her cheeks, fixing Gina with a look that said she would bet a million dollars her ex wouldn't get the answer right.

"*Elf*, of course," Gina answered triumphantly as Sophia pummeled her with the throw pillow. It bounced harmlessly to the floor. "Which should have been a sign. Clearly, you were always meant to star in Christmas movies."

"It's April!" Sophia argued, shifting her legs so

that they inched closer to Gina's. Her eyes darted to the pillow on the floor as if belatedly realizing it was gone.

"So?" Gina kept her eyes fixed on Sophia's face, refusing to stare at the less than half an inch of empty space that separated them. "You're filming a holiday flick. It'll help you stay in character."

"I *was* filming." A trace of dejectedness crept back into Sophia's tone. "Who knows what tomorrow will bring?"

"They haven't closed you down yet, so no past tense." When Sophia failed to perk back up after a few seconds, Gina added, "Tell you what. I'll agree to let you take that old screenplay of mine to read. But you have to promise me one thing."

Interest kindled in Sophia's eyes. "What's that?"

"Burn it once you've finished." Gina rose from the couch and crossed to her desk, fishing the printed manuscript from the drawer, right where she'd known it would be.

She dropped it into Sophia's lap, flopping back onto the couch. Somehow, though she hadn't intended for it to happen, that tiny space that had existed between their bodies was gone. Instead of pulling away, Sophia slipped the screenplay into her shoulder bag before reaching for a blanket. She spread it across them both to share, as they'd done so many times in the past.

"Thank you." Sophia slipped further under the

blanket, heat from her body seeping beneath Gina's skin like a furnace set on high.

"I'm serious about that script." Gina pointed the remote at the TV and turned it on, scrolling to find the movie in her streaming options. "It isn't fit for anyone else's eyes but yours."

CHAPTER TEN

Sophia floated on a cloud in the darkness, every inch of her body existing in a perfect state of relaxation. She breathed in slowly, the scent of spicy musk bringing a wave of comfort to her being, like coming home after a lifetime away.

As consciousness chased away the cobwebs in her brain, Sophia stiffened without moving, her eyes flying open. The unfamiliar room surrounding her was filled with gray shadows, illuminated by just enough light to indicate the sun was thinking about coming up but hadn't yet committed. As for that perfect pillow she'd been resting her head on, it was not a pillow at all. It was Gina.

Sophia barely dared to breathe as she assessed the situation. They were in Gina's apartment. That much she remembered. From what she could tell, they'd fallen asleep on the couch while watching *Elf* the night before. When exactly that had happened was a mystery, but since even the television screensaver had gone black, several hours must have passed. The blanket Sophia had draped over them remained in place, and she could feel the heat of Gina's fingers pressed into her shoulder, cradling her close like a beloved teddy bear.

Every memory came flooding back of all the times she'd woken like this before, safe in Gina's arms. How often had she dreamed herself here over the years, only to find herself alone in an empty bed? But this seemed real, if only for the moment. Sophia didn't want to leave, or move, or even breathe.

It has to be past five, nagged the rational voice in her head, the one responsible for getting her punctually to work.

She was expected on set at six. Fortunately, though it was a twenty-minute drive from Gina's place back to Sholan Falls, Sophia didn't need to change or do her hair or makeup. It was a *come as you a*re type of arrangement on filming days. All she had to do was roll out of bed and go. Or roll off the couch, as the case might be.

Holding her breath, Sophia allowed herself one last moment to soak in Gina's nearness. The woman slept soundly, not seeming to notice as Sophia stirred. So peaceful. It was a beautiful sight, Gina's hair like a dark cloud around her head, a sweet half smile on her lips. Sophia stared at them as she inched away, wondering if she dared leave a kiss on them as she once would've done.

Better not, said that stupid, rational voice again. Sophia was baffled. Actors were hardly known, as a whole, for being a levelheaded bunch. Where had it come from, and why was it so insistent on being obeyed?

With a sigh, Sophia gathered up the empty takeout containers and chopsticks from the ottoman and whisked them to the kitchen. Tidying up was a very distant second to kissing on her list of ways to show affection, but it would have to do. Fortunately, the rest of the leftovers had made it into the refrigerator sometime the night before, so there was little else to do but run a cleaning wipe over the table and counter before heading out.

As Sophia gently closed the front door behind her, Gina continued to sleep.

When Sophia made her way to the wardrobe trailer a few minutes before six, the town common was eerily quiet. She climbed the steps to the trailer door, but when she turned the knob, she found it locked. She surveyed the set uneasily. Had she missed something? She'd been in such a rush to get here on time from Gina's she hadn't checked for messages. As she reached for her phone, she spotted Matt coming toward her.

"There's the woman I'm looking for," Matt called up from the base of the trailer steps.

"What's going on?" Sophia tried to ignore the rush of adrenaline that made her fingers tingle. "Did I miss something? This place looks like a ghost town."

"There's been a change of plans. Filming is suspended today, but you're wanted for a meeting."

"Right now?" Sophia gripped her shoulder bag for support.

Matt shook his head. "Not until ten, in a private meeting room at O'Malley's. I guess they tried calling you last night, but you didn't pick up, and they didn't want to leave a message."

"They?" Sophia cringed as she realized she'd put her ringer on silent while she was at Gina's, not that she would've answered anyway, unless she recognized the number.

"Someone from IBC Entertainment in LA," Matt said with a *whoop-de-do* finger waggle. "Not sure who. Way above my pay grade. I was just asked to come over here at six, find you, and give you the message."

IBC Entertainment? That could mean only one thing. The suits were on their way. Sophia thanked the few lucky stars she might still have hanging out in the sky above her that she'd at least have time to go back to the inn and change. The only thing worse than a bunch of network executives canceling her contract and dashing her dreams for the future was for them to do it while she was still dressed like she was doing a walk of shame.

Sophia's head spun as she contemplated the

possible reasons for this last-minute meeting. Only one made sense. "This is it, isn't it? They're shutting us down."

Matt didn't respond, but it was obvious looking at his face that he held the same opinion.

Sophia went back to the inn for a shower and reemerged a little before ten, dressed like a star, as she entered the Irish pub that was Sholan Fall's one restaurant that had private rooms available for meetings and parties. It was much too early for the restaurant to be open to diners, and when she walked through the doors, the owner stood alone at the front, sending her in the correct direction with a nod.

As Sophia approached the sliding doors that separated the small banquet room from the rest of the pub, dread sloshed deep in her belly. At a long table that could accommodate twelve sat a man she had never met in person but recognized instantly from photos in the LA papers. Ken Abrams, head of entertainment for IBC. Next to him sat a statuesque middle-aged woman whose dark brown hair was pulled back into a knot at the nape of her neck. She, too, looked familiar, but Sophia couldn't put a name to the face.

They were the only two in the room, looking so polished and professional Sophia was once again grateful she'd had a chance to change. Her wide legged trousers and sweater twin set gave her the confidence to enter the room that yoga pants and a hoodie could never replicate.

"Am I early?" Sophia asked through pursed lips, certain she was right on time. "Where's Mr. Dix?"

"Sophia!" Ken got to his feet, his arms wide for an embrace, but then he realized a table blocked him from an actual hug, much to Sophia's relief. He was probably the type to kiss both cheeks, which made Sophia beyond nervous, despite her Italian family. She always got confused and feared one day she would kiss a stranger smack dab on the lips.

"Mr. Abrams, this is an honor." Sophia was thrilled that she sounded truly honored instead of petrified.

"The honor is all mine." He retook his seat, and it did not escape Sophia's attention that he still had not answered her question regarding the producer's glaring absence. "Let me introduce Jill Davidson—"

Sophia experienced a Eureka moment and blurted, "Oh, wow, of course!"

"You know Jill?" Ken knitted his brow, though it was hard to tell if he was perplexed or impressed by this revelation.

"Jill Davidson, Head of Sapphicsticated, Inc.? You bet." Sophia said it so fast she had to stop to catch her breath. "I'm a huge admirer. Ms. Davidson."

"Well, that's really sweet," Jill replied, a faint blush on her cheeks. "And quite unexpected."

Sophia turned to Ken, unable to stop herself from adding, "Did you know she started as an associate producer at Grant Studios before becoming one of the founding members of the largest production company in the United States dedicated to positive lesbian content?"

"It's not often I have my resume recited to me." Jill laughed at her own joke, but she couldn't hide the fact Sophia had obviously scored some points, even though that hadn't been her intention.

"You're probably wondering why we're here," Ken began, before pausing to point to the carafe and mugs in the center of the table. "Do you want some coffee? Come take a seat."

"Yes to the coffee," Sophia said, approaching the table and pouring herself a cup. She settled into one of the chairs across from him and Jill. "As for why you're here, I don't know, but I think I can guess. Butch?"

"I won't lie. The Butch situation is a total disaster. We watched the dailies, and I can't imagine what Holden thought he was doing." Ken tapped a finger on the table cloth. "He's gone, by the way. And Butch."

I'm next. Sophia swallowed, praying her thoughts didn't show on her face. "Gone, as in replaced? Or..." Did they cancel both of their multi-deal contracts?

"That remains to be seen." Ken twisted his head to look at Jill. "That's why we've brought Jill in, to see what can be salvaged, and why I wanted to see you, as one of the producers we haven't fired."

Did the word *yet* hang over Sophia's head? Wanting to push this fear out of the way, Sophia focused on Jill. "I didn't realize you worked with IBC," Sophia said, trying to work out why Jill, of all people, was there.

"I didn't until this week," Jill responded. "The official announcement is yet to be made, but as of yesterday, IBC has acquired a controlling interest in Sapphicsticated."

"Jill has been promoted to an executive position within IBC Entertainment," Ken added.

"But that's..." Sophia grinned. "That's amazing. Are you here to take over the film?"

"Not the day to day, but as executive producer, maybe," Jill said.

"If there's a film to take over," Ken added, sending Sophia's spirits plummeting.

"Oh." Sophia clutched her coffee mug to steady her nerves. "What can I do to help?"

Jill let out a breath. "I've only glanced at the script, but I'm not going to sugarcoat this. It's fucking crap."

Sophia found herself nodding. It was. No need to argue.

"Can we fix it, though?" Ken stroked his chin.

"The script—no way." Jill looked like she might gag. "I don't know why Dix green lit such a ghastly story."

"And, we all know Butch should be in traction, not on a movie set," Ken tossed in, just to bring Sophia's hopes a little lower. "Too bad because he's perfect for these movies."

"The way I see it, we have two things going for us. Sophia"—Jill motioned to her as she said this, making it clear that the actor herself was number one on the list of assets—"and the town itself, which is absolutely Christmas magic. Even so, we'd be starting almost from square one with the need to assign a new producer and write an entirely new script, not to mention we're down by one male lead."

"IBC has already invested a million in this project," Ken said, not making it clear whether this was an argument for or against shutting down the project.

"There's nothing you can do about the sunk costs, but there's also no point throwing good money after bad." There was no question where Jill seemed to stand on the issue. Sophia's hopes for her first big production and a future with IBC dimmed by the second.

"Do we have a backup script?" Ken demanded, wringing his hands until the knuckles turned white.

Tears stinging her eyes, Sophia glanced down to avoid the executives catching her on the verge of crying. Her gaze landed on her shoulder bag, and as she remembered what was inside, her pulse ticked faster.

Sophia dipped a hand into her bag but hesitated. Gina had said no one could read it but Sophia.

Jill shook her head. "This is IBC's first Christmas movie. There may be one or two in the pipeline but nowhere near the same ballpark as the channels that churn out these movies."

"How quickly could our writers bash one out?"

"Not fast enough," Jill replied.

Ken let out a huff of air. "I don't know what to do then, except to close down—"

"Wait!" The threat of the ax coming down for good was enough to spur Sophia into action. She whipped out Gina's script, vowing to think about the consequences later. Right now, she had a movie to save. "I have this."

"What is it?" Jill asked. Both she and Ken peered over the table as Jill read the title. "*Christmas in Rainbow Falls*. Did you write it?"

"Me? No." Sophia laughed nervously. "A professor at Comstock College, Gina Mitchells, wrote it. She's a documentary filmmaker, but also a brilliant screenwriter. She wrote it to be set right here in Sholan Falls, so the set could be used exactly as it is. I'm betting most of the actors could simply be recast into similar roles in the new script, costumes would stay the same. It could be up and running before you know it."

"Except, we'll need at least a week to rehearse the new script," Jill argued. "Best case, we're two weeks behind schedule, leaving what, four weeks to shoot an entire movie?"

As the woman started to laugh at the ridiculousness of such a task, Sophia felt compelled to say, "I can tell you from experience you only need three weeks to film one of these movies."

"Three?" Ken stroked his chin.

"Fifteen days of filming. Trust me. They don't call me the Queen of Christmas for nothing." Sophia held her breath, expecting to be laughed out of the room. Instead, both executives continued to flip through the script, clearly willing to give Sophia's Hail Mary at least a moment of consideration.

"*Rainbow Falls*," Ken said the words slowly as if trying to decipher the meaning, or maybe hoping for his own miracle that it wasn't as gay as it sounded.

Sophia had some bad news for him if that was the case.

"It's a sapphic rom-com," she confirmed. "But it's not the typical story you see on TV with two female leads. Neither of them dies, for one thing. There's no great angst about coming out to family. It's your ordinary Christmas story—"

"But with two female leads?" Ken pressed.

"Yes, but, maybe one could be changed." Sophia wanted to throw herself off a cliff for suggesting it, knowing Gina would kill her. But if a compromise was what was needed to save the production...

"Don't you dare change it," Jill interjected, looking giddy. "That is exactly the type of programming IBC was looking for in partnering with my company."

"You might be right." A smile spread across Ken's face as the possibilities sank in. "That's how we'll differentiate ourselves from the other channels. But what if the script's a dud?"

"If you'll pardon me for saying it," Sophia broke in, "almost anything would be heads above the one you were already planning to produce with Dix."

"And this one would have no dicks, which is already an improvement as far as I'm concerned," Jill said dryly. She pressed her lips together thoughtfully. "I'll tell you what. I'll take this script and give it a look over the next few days. If I think I can make it work, I'll green light it."

Sophia had to hold onto her seat to keep from jumping up and cheering. The production was possibly saved, and along with it, her future at IBC. She couldn't wait to tell Gina the good news. After all these years, Gina's dream of seeing one of her sapphic rom-coms make it to the screen might be coming true.

CHAPTER ELEVEN

Gina stretched her neck, tilting her head from one side to another as a yawn escaped. There wasn't enough coffee in the universe. It had been a rough night, plagued by dreams she hadn't had in years. Not bad dreams—quite the opposite, filled with happy images of her and Sophia together—but painful, all the same. Waking up to find herself alone hadn't helped. She wasn't sure when Sophia had left. Gina only knew that by the time she'd raised herself up from the couch, stiff and exhausted, Sophia had slipped out without saying a word.

And Gina had been running late. No matter, though. She'd made up for it by working nonstop from the moment she set foot in the office. It was possible working twice as hard as usual would wipe all trace of the previous night's dreams from her mind. She hadn't been this productive in forever.

Rolling backward in her chair, Gina admired her clean desk. She hadn't seen the grains in the wood for weeks. For someone always enmeshed in chaos, Gina preferred everything to be orderly. Late at night, when she couldn't sleep, she dreamed of all the ways she'd organize everything in her life. Starting at home, she pictured shelves for all her canned goods. Cubbies for all of her paperwork. Her wardrobe hanging up in the closet, sorted by colors.

Everything would have a place, and she'd never feel overwhelmed by bedlam.

In reality, her cupboards were a nightmare, with bags of black beans piled on top of soup cans and boxes of pasta in at least three separate locations. Every letter, notebook, exam, and scrap of paper that had ever entered her orbit were stuffed in drawers or piled wherever. The closest her clothes came to being organized were in three piles. Clean. Decent. Dirty.

But in this moment, Gina was reveling in a major accomplishment. She'd finished grading exams. All of them. They'd even been handed back to the students. The end of the semester was in sight. Her next big project was to finish the promo piece on Professor Harlowe's documentary.

Er... *their* documentary. Gina was an equal partner in the project, though sometimes it was hard to see it that way because she struggled most days to view herself as a proper adult and not one pretending like she had her shit together. If her mentor had a hard time remembering sometimes that Gina was no longer his teaching assistant, but a fellow faculty member on mostly equal footing, he wasn't the only one to blame. Gina forgot sometimes, too.

"Got a second?" As if conjured by thoughts about him, the department head spoke from the doorway, clutching a stack of papers to his chest. He wore a three-piece suit with a bow tie, giving Gina the impression he was headed somewhere special.

"Of course." Gina leaned back in her chair, threading her fingers behind her head.

"You look relaxed."

"I finished all my grading," Gina explained, indulging in a final stretch before sitting upright. "I love that feeling."

"That's exactly why I came to you," the professor said, suddenly sounding breathless. "I have to head out of town for a follow-up interview—"

"For the documentary?" Gina's eyes narrowed slightly as she considered the man's attire for a second time. Didn't he always wear all black when he went into the field?

"Yes. That scene that's been troubling me for the promo piece for investors—you know the one. Well, I figured out what's wrong. I didn't ask the right follow-up question, so I'm going to do that."

Gina's shoulders tensed. "That scene has been finalized. You told me two weeks ago to go ahead and work with what we had."

"I know, but…" Evan Harlowe hitched a shoulder helplessly, as if he weren't the one calling the shots, which he most certainly was. "Since I have to do that, I was hoping you could grade these exams for me." He proceeded to dump a stack of papers onto Gina's recently cleared desk. "Gotta run!"

No sooner had he delivered the news than the professor was out the door. Gina didn't even have time to say she couldn't grade the papers because she had to finish the promo piece, which apparently was still very much a work in progress despite having ostensibly finalized what would go in the portion for Pride. Leave it to Evan, who by the way, continually pestered Gina about getting the thing done.

Gina rubbed her temples as she surveyed the stack of term papers. Every single time she started to get ahead, something dragged her back. Whether it was work, or finally putting her anguish over Sophia in the past, the universe seemed hellbent on undermining all her hard work.

Her stomach churned, and the start of a migraine pounded behind her left eye as the anxiety she'd managed to hold at bay with her office purge came spilling over the edge of her too-short dam. Gina balled her fists, barely refraining from smacking them against the surface of her once-empty desk.

Someone tapped on the door.

Ah, geezus. What new task had Harlowe forgotten to dump on her now and sent someone to deliver the news? Gina nearly blew her stack, and it was all she could do not to scream *Fuck off! Everyone should die and leave me alone. Right now.*

"Yes," she growled through gritted teeth instead.

But a moment later, it was Sophia whose head came into view. Despite being the source of so much inner turmoil, this woman was also possibly the only person on the planet who could calm Gina when she was in her *everyone should die and leave me alone* mood. The pang of guilt was instant.

"What's wrong?" Instead of being scared away by Gina's greeting, Sophia sank onto the lip of the desk.

"It's just—it's nothing."

"No. It's not nothing." Sophia placed a hand on Gina's shoulder, massaging.

Gina closed her eyes, sinking into that feeling. Couldn't they stay exactly like this forever? No future or past to worry about, just closeness and peace.

Gina sighed before she let her frustrations come spilling out. "Harlowe just dumped these exams for me to grade so he could dash out of town to redo an interview that's already gone through post-production, which took me about a week."

Sophia's jaw clenched. "I see Evan Harlowe hasn't changed one bit."

"What does that mean?" Gina pulled back from Sophia's touch, snapping before she could stop herself. For someone who was normally as sweet as a cartoon princess, Sophia's tone had a noticeable lack of warmth when she spoke of Gina's mentor. Belatedly, Gina recalled Sophia had taken classes from the man in college and hadn't seemed too fond of him even then. Sure, the man loved to name drop and such, but hadn't he earned the right given his success and being such a champion for marginalized communities?

"When you were his teacher's assistant back in college, he was always putting you in bad spots. Doing all the grading. The slicing and dicing in the editing room. Hell, he even had you bring him coffee in the morning and pick up his dry cleaning."

"He paid me for that extra work," Gina defended, even though she knew she had never once asked her own GAs to do anything remotely similar. Nor would she ever cross that line.

"Peanuts," Sophia argued. Whether she meant it to or not, Sophia's derisiveness immediately put Gina on the offensive, as if she was the one to blame for her professor's lack of boundaries.

"It helped me make ends meet," Gina argued, heat building inside her like a pressure cooker. "Besides, if it wasn't for Harlowe, I wouldn't have gotten this far. He's the one who set me up for the internship in New York when my dream fell apart."

"What are you talking about? Your dream didn't fall apart," Sophia scoffed, giving a soft snort as if the words didn't compute. "You *changed* your dream. Though it wouldn't surprise me if that man had a hand in that."

"Is that what you think?" All at once, every ounce of frustration and anger that had been building within her burst, and Gina was powerless to hold anything back. "That's really rich, considering it was your former employer that was to blame for pulverizing my vision of the future."

"What?" Sophia stared blankly, her face the picture of a wounded animal. "Because they hired me?"

"No." Gina waved a hand to dismiss this idea, though not with nearly the amount of compassion she might've shown under other circumstances. "Don't you remember when Alex Cross from Keynote came to campus during the career fair?"

"Yes, of course, I remember." It was clear Sophia wasn't seeing any connection to what happened a short time after, when Gina gave up her screenwriting dreams for good. How had Sophia never guessed? Bitterness settled over Gina like a damp wool blanket. Sophia was supposed to have known Gina better than anyone, but the woman never picked up on that?

"Cross," Gina said, nearly spitting as she said the cursed name aloud, "made it clear that a Black lesbian wanting to write rom-coms would never get anywhere in a mostly straight, white world."

Sophia sucked in her breath, her expression morphing to one of pure pain, as if Gina had dealt her a physical blow. "Why didn't you tell me?"

"Because you were on cloud nine." Gina's eyes burned with tears as it all came rushing over her, drowning her. "Because you'd been told you were perfect Keynote material, and they wanted you in LA the day after graduation."

"But—I wouldn't have taken a job with them if I'd known that!"

"I know!" Gina heard herself shout, but it didn't register that the sound had come from her. Now that it had been set free, she was too far gone with long buried emotions to do anything to stop the flood of foulness seeping from every pore. "It's why I didn't tell you. Loyalty was always one of your strongest attributes, even when it would be your undoing. I couldn't have that on my conscience"

"That's why you dumped me, isn't it?" Sophia sprang off the desk, pacing Gina's small office. "You thought you were saving me."

"I didn't want to get in your way."

"You were never in my way, Gina Mitchells," Sophia seethed, her eyes flashing warning. "But by keeping that from me... I don't even know what to say."

"You can't be too surprised." Gina's words came out way harsher than she'd intended, not that it mattered at this point. If there was any damage left to do, she might as well get it done. "You might think IBC is more open-minded, but they've still given you that *don't be overly gay* clause. And you didn't even fight it. But sure, lecture me about my boss."

"Not anymore, damn it." Sophia stomped her foot,

looking like she wished Gina's head had been beneath it. "That's what I came by to tell you. I have the best news."

"You're allowed to be bisexual?" Gina guessed.

Sophia's eyes narrowed. "Stop being such a jerk, or I'll leave without telling you."

"Fine." Gina crossed her arms but refrained from digging her hole any deeper. For now. "What did you come here to say?"

"Keynote didn't realize how gifted you are, but I always knew." Despite the tension between them, some of the worry seemed to ease from Sophia's brow. "And IBC can spot the Real McCoy."

The pressure behind Gina's eye had doubled, her head throbbing all over as she tried and failed to figure out what the fuck Sophia was trying to say. "I have no idea what you're talking about."

"It's like you said. Your dream of writing rom-coms with people like you in them." As Sophia grew more animated, her pitch went higher, sending a shard of pain into Gina's brain.

"People like me?"

"I'm not saying this right." Sophia waved her hands in frustration, though it seemed mostly directed at herself. "I'm not trying to be an asshole, really. It's just, what you said… it's a lot to take in. But, we can talk about that later. What I came to tell you now is there's a good chance IBC will want to option your script."

"What script?"

"*Christmas at Rainbow Falls.*" Sophia studied her with an expectant gaze, clearly waiting on a reaction.

All Gina could see was a glowing red somewhere behind her retinas. "You pitched my story to IBC?" she whispered.

"Actually, I..." For the first time, Sophia showed hesitance. "I... um... gave them your script."

Gina's breaths came quick and shallow. "The script I said to burn after reading?"

"It's too good to b—" Sophia began, but Gina couldn't listen to another syllable. Fear, anger, and pain jockeyed for first position within her burning chest.

Gina squeezed her eyes shut. "Remember earlier when I said loyalty was one of your best traits? I was wrong."

"Gina—"

"I *trusted* you," Gina lashed out, barely coherent as her head—and the whole world—seemed to spin out of control.

"Gina!" Sophia pleaded as Gina hovered on the edge of hyperventilating.

"I explicitly said to burn it. Not to show anyone. I wrote it ten years ago. Now you're standing in my office, proud of yourself. I'll be completely humiliated. Oh—" It hit her in a flash what this had to be. What other explanation was there? "This is my payback for breaking your heart. Have you been planning this since graduation?"

"Planning *what?*" Sophia's tone was chilly.

"To make me suffer even more than I already have. Breaking up with you was the hardest thing I've ever done. I could barely get the words out, but I knew it was best for you."

"Oh, don't even try that." Sophia spat out.

Even Gina, through the haze of paranoid anger that had engulfed her, could tell that sounded like crazy talk. Too late to fix it, Gina feared she'd gone too far.

"You broke up with me because you were too proud to tell me the truth. You didn't do it for me. You did it for *yourself*."

"Sophia, that's—"

"If you really think I've put all these balls into play simply to crush your screenwriting dream—what the *fuck* is wrong with you?" Tears streamed down Sophia's cheeks, and she made no move to wipe them away. "I came here today with what I thought was good news, and all you can see is some nefarious conspiracy!"

Before Gina could break out of the paralysis that had overtaken her, Sophia had turned on one heel and marched from her office.

"I wish you'd never come back into my life!" Gina screamed before collapsing into tears on her desktop as the pile of ungraded term papers flew to the floor.

CHAPTER TWELVE

IN THE SPACIOUS, SUN-FILLED LOUNGE OF THE health spa where she was spending the afternoon, Sophia collapsed onto a towel-draped chaise, her mother on one side of her and little sister Carrie on the other. Sophia plucked at her thick terry robe, pulling it from each side toward the middle to better cover her bare legs and the bathing suit that was still damp from the hot tub.

"Isn't this the life?" Her mom sipped water infused with fruit slices. "I've never had a spa day with all of my girls before."

Sophia opened her mouth to offer a perfunctory *you're welcome,* since the outing was her treat, but before she could say anything, Carrie jumped in to add, "That's because *one* of us is never home to participate in girls' day out."

"Hey," Sophia said but didn't follow it up with anything more substantial.

The truth was, she didn't have the energy to fight, not even with her sister, which was a rarity. But dragging herself through the past forty-eight hours of uncertainty had been hell on two fronts, and all because of one script.

Gina wasn't speaking to Sophia after the blowout—not a single text. And instead of coming back with an offer right away like Sophia had hoped, Jill had gone radio silent. All of which was why launching into an argument about the five million reasons it was impossible for her to fly all the way across the country for monthly spa days threatened to do Sophia in once and for all.

"You've barely said a peep since we got here." As if sensing her mood, her mom pressed, "What's wrong?"

"Nothing," Sophia protested, though only half-heartedly. "It's not easy talking in the steam room, and don't get me started on the Himalayan salt room. I'll be tasting it until I die." Sophia pretended hacking up salt wedged deep in her throat.

"Not buying it." Her mom crossed her arms. "Something else is going on."

"I don't buy it, either." Carrie nudged Sophia's leg with a bare foot. "No one was in the steam room with us. Mom and I talked the whole time."

No kidding. Frankly, Sophia was surprised they'd noticed her silence.

"Come on," her mom urged. "I never get to hear about your life. You owe me."

"Did I get that trait from you?" Sophia asked, amazed at how her mom could somehow weaponize showing support.

"Being quiet?" her mom guessed.

"No." Sophia choked back a laugh. "Not that. I was talking about guilt trips."

"I don't do that," her mom protested.

As Sophia's lips twitched, Carrie burst into a laughing fit but quickly pretended she choked on a lime wedge in her water.

After giving Carrie an evil side eye, Sophia's mom asked, "Is this about Gina?"

"Uh—?" Sophia's brain sputtered as she tried to figure out what her mom meant by that question. Had she guessed they'd had a fight? Or had she guessed they'd never been together in the first place? She wasn't sure what to do.

"Nothing's wrong with Gina." Why didn't Sophia cancel girls' day out? Yes, she was an actor, but pretending everything was hunky dory after the dustup with Gina two days prior? It was too taxing, even for her. This was a far cry from pretending to shiver on a ninety-degree summer's day.

"Your voice did that thing when you lie!" Carrie jabbed an accusing finger in Sophia's direction.

"What thing?" Sophia squeaked.

"That thing!" her sister insisted. "It sounds like you sucked on a helium balloon."

"It does not!" Even as she said it, Sophia could hear how it sounded exactly as her sister described.

Now her mother was wagging a finger at Sophia like she was a naughty puppy. "There it is again!"

"I should have gone with Bella." The only thing worse than being miserable alone was being miserable with other people around and trying to pretend you weren't.

"Bella's having a prenatal massage. Unless…" Her mom's face lit up in the most comical way. "Are you saying—"

"Are you joking?" This time, Sophia noticed her denial was not the least bit helium-filled. Probably a good thing. "How would that even—no, never mind. I refuse to explain the birds and the bees to my own mother."

"Or, would it be the birds and the birds?" Carrie pondered, stroking her chin. "The bees and the bees?"

"Don't strain yourself trying to figure it out." Sophia rolled her eyes. "It doesn't matter, anyway. There aren't any birds or bees."

"Why would you say that?" Sophia's mom asked.

"Because I'm pretty sure I'm the worst person on the planet. Gina certainly thinks so, anyway."

Her mom and Carrie exchanged a conspiratorial head nod as if they knew the good stuff was finally on its way.

"What'd you do this time?" her mom demanded.

"Nothing…" Sophia protested, but not with her usual vehemence. It was mostly out of habit, for all the times her mom assumed she'd been at fault when the opposite was true. Right now, her mom had a point. "When I showed Gina's script to my producer, I thought I was doing something good."

Her mother's face went blank. Whatever juicy gossip she'd been anticipating, this clearly was not it.

"I don't get it," Carrie chimed in. "What does a script have to do with anything?"

"It'd always been Gina's dream, before she… before we broke up—"

"It's okay," Carrie said. "We know she dumped you."

"It was on the news," her mom added dryly.

"Fine," Sophia pouted. "Yes. She did. She dumped me to make documentaries, or so I thought, because they were more important than the frivolous things I wanted to do."

"That doesn't sound like Gina," her mom said haltingly, a whisper of doubt creeping into her tone.

"For once, Mom, you're right," Sophia confirmed. She clenched her hands as the anger and frustration of the last few days started to mount. "As it turns out, she lied about that, because—get this"—Sophia made eye contact with her mom and then swiveled to eyeball Carrie—"she says she sacrificed our relationship for *my* sake. So I could go to LA and audition for

Keystone Channel instead of following her to New York."

"You never would've made it half as far in New York," Carrie pointed out, most unhelpfully.

"That's not the point." Sophia glared at her sister. "I never asked her to do that. I didn't even know about it. And I'm such an idiot, because here I thought our fake dating arrangement was actually *leading* somewhere. Like we'd be able to find our way back to how we were, but apparently that was all a facade, too—I don't know. It's hard to know what happened, because I still can't believe it. Not to mention I haven't gotten a wink of sleep in forty-eight hours."

By the time she reached the end of her tirade, Sophia was shaking from head to toe, tears spilling down her cheeks.

"Fake dating. Facade. No sleep." Her mom pronounced each word carefully, lifting one eyebrow in exactly the same gesture Sophia often used in similar situations. "I think we need to hear this whole story from the beginning, Let's try the whole truth and nothing but the truth this time, so we can help you."

"I just did!" Unable to stomp because she was still reclined on the chaise, Sophia kicked her feet like a two-year-old having a tantrum.

"Maybe go through it once more," Carrie urged, sounding surprisingly sympathetic. "Remember, we thought you broke up with Gina until we heard otherwise oh so recently. We're playing catch-up."

"Please, Sophia." Her mom's expression was earnest and loving, piercing Sophia's heart. "Let us in."

Still sniffling, Sophia took a deep breath. She closed her eyes and started at the beginning, all the way back to when she'd first met Gina. She'd known that first day they were meant to be together. As she retold it, despite everything that had happened since that day, Sophia felt it even more deeply now.

When Sophia finished, she was on the verge of ugly crying. "I really did think this time it'd work."

Neither her sister nor her mom said a thing for a very long second. Sophia noted with surprise that sometime during all of this, Bella had returned and was seated on one of the cushioned rocking chairs. Sophia had been so wrapped up in talking, she hadn't noticed.

It was her mom who finally broke the silence. "It sounds like that movie. What is it called?"

"*Sleepless in Seattle?*" Carrie suggested while Bella nodded.

"No," her mom said, waving her hand. "The other one, with Deborah Kerr and Cary Grant."

"What movie?" Sophia asked impatiently. After ripping open her chest and letting her guts spill out all over the spa, were they really going to start discussing movies like a film club? "What are you even talking about?"

"You remember," Bella said. "They're supposed to

meet at the top of the Empire State Building, but then she ends up in a wheelchair, and she decides she doesn't want to force Grant into keeping his word. What's the name of it? It's on the tip of my tongue."

"*An Affair to Remember!*" Carrie yelled, following it up with a triumphant whoop, like she was a game show contestant who'd just won a prize.

"Are you all serious right now?" Sophia asked in disbelief. Although why she was in shock, she wasn't sure. This was her family, through and through. Totally crazy but kind of sweet, nonetheless.

"I've watched that movie so many times," Bella added, "and it still makes me cry."

Seriously. If they didn't get to the point, Sophia was going to be the one crying. Again. "Life isn't like a movie. I'm talking about real life. How does this relate?"

"Don't you see?" Sophia's mom asked, frowning when Sophia shook her head. "Gina loves you so much that she was trying to spare you from making a bad decision she knew would hurt you."

"By hurting me?" Sophia demanded, every inch of her tingling with raw nerves. "I'm calling baloney on that one. She could have talked to me. We could have worked something out. She's practically been living right down the street this whole time, apparently. She's had ten years to spill the beans."

"When?" Carrie prodded. "It's not like you're ever around. Not even for Christmas."

Sophia cradled her head with both hands, wishing this conversation would miraculously end. She'd do anything for some silence, even brave the salt room again. But there was no escaping the females in her family. They were as relentless as lionesses on a hunt. "Oh, sure. I'm the Queen of Christmas, right? But you want to know the truth? I'm starting to hate the stupid holiday. I spend most of the year pretending it's Christmas, celebrating with strangers I don't care about, and when the actual day arrives, I'm always so flipping exhausted. Do you want to know what I do every Christmas? I sleep. And cry. Sleep. Cry. I'm single. I can't even have a pet, unless you count all the cobwebs in my apartment, because I'm never home long enough to take care of anything."

"You don't have to be single," her mother said softly. "Especially now when it's so clear how much Gina still loves you."

Sophia swallowed, tasting nothing but bitterness. "Yeah, she loves me so much she threw me out of her office and hasn't spoken to me since."

Instead of sympathy, her mom gave her that familiar look, the one that said she was about to figure out where her daughter had gone wrong and then inform her of it in stark detail. "How many times have you called?"

Sophia clenched her teeth. "None."

"Texted?"

Sophia shook her head.

"Email?" This time her mom squeaked.

"Is that the helium voice?" Sophia asked Carrie.

"Similar," her sister confirmed. "I'll take your sudden shifting of the conversation to mean that's a big fat no on the email."

"You two graduated from college a decade ago, but neither of you has done much growing up." Her mom's voice revved as if preparing to drive her point home. Sophia braced for it. "Do you know what you two need to do? You need to talk."

"Mom—"

But Sophia's mom ignored her, jabbing a finger at Sophia's phone. "Send her a text right now, saying you need to talk."

"No one ever wants to receive a text that says *we need to talk*," Sophia argued. "That's, like, science or something."

"I don't care how you phrase it," her mother argued back. "The fact remains communicating is exactly what you need to do. That's what being a grown-up entails. That and laundry. A lot of laundry."

Sophia chuckled at her mom's silly attempt at a joke, choking on her own snot and realizing she'd been blubbering nonstop for at least fifteen minutes.

"Send her a text," Bella urged, taking their mom's side, naturally. Although Sophia suspected maybe they both had a point.

She still had to fight them on it, of course. "I can't—"

Her mom turned to Carrie, who stood, looking oddly menacing for a woman wearing a terry robe and fluffy slippers with a white towel on her head.

Sophia cowered, recalling every tussle they'd ever gotten into as kids. "What are you going to do?"

Instead of answering with words, Carrie demonstrated by sitting on Sophia, pinning her down. Bella, nearly tipping over from her protruding belly, took the opportunity to rifle through the pockets of Sophia's bathrobe. She squealed when she located the phone. "Got it. If Soph won't text Gina, we'll do it for her."

"Give it back!" Sophia hollered. She wiggled, trying to free herself, but Carrie dug in. Sophia changed tactics, trying to use logic to persuade the three clearly irrational women she was somehow related to. "It won't do you any good. You can't unlock it without a passcode."

"Oh, really?" Her mom rose to her feet, seized the phone, and held it in front of Sophia's face, instantly unlocking the screen. "I bet you didn't think your mom knew how all that new-fangled technology worked, did you?"

Sophia stuck out her tongue. It was true. She had underestimated her mom and would pay the price. "Can't we be adult about this?"

"Finally!" Her mom grinned. "That's all I'm asking, for you and Gina to act like adults. I'm going to give you one more chance. Text Gina and tell her you want to discuss what's gone on between you, or I will."

Nostrils flaring, at least in some part because Carrie still had not let her up and she was running short on breath, Sophia reached for the phone. She typed in a text as directed and hit send.

"I want it on the record that I hate all of you," Sophia muttered as her sister finally released her. "If this goes poorly, I blame you all completely."

"You don't hate us," Sophia's mom said lightly, her eyes full of the type of merriment that never let Sophia stay mad at her for long. "As for it going poorly, I don't see how you two could make any bigger a mess of things than you already have, so I'm willing to take my chances."

Great, Sophia thought. Her mother was willing to take chances with Sophia's pathetic love life, but was Sophia ready to do the same?

CHAPTER THIRTEEN

WE HAVE TO TALK.

Was Gina wrong to think that was the worst sentence in the English language?

Sure, *you need a root canal* wasn't a great thing to be told, either. But at least it provided information. You knew what you were looking at when a sentence like that was said. That wasn't the case with *we have to talk*. That was a real heart-stopper. Without additional context, *we have to talk* left the recipient free to imagine every worst-case scenario under the sun.

Which was exactly what Gina had been doing for the past twenty-four hours.

As she stood in the parking lot of Boo's Burgers, shifting her weight from one foot to the other, she pretended her only care in the world was checking out the beautiful blue sky overhead. In reality, every car that drove by caused her heart to spasm as she waited for Sophia to arrive.

The text had said four o'clock. Sophia was running late.

Or maybe she'd decided they didn't need to talk after all. Maybe all of their talking days were done, destroyed by Gina's foul mood and complete lack of filter when frustrated. Gina really couldn't blame Sophia if that was the case. Things had been said that couldn't be unsaid, and no *I'm sorry*—a far superior sentence to *we have to talk* but still with its limitations—couldn't begin to cover.

When Sophia finally did appear three minutes later, her arrival took Gina, who was busy making a list of the best and worst English sentences she could think of and putting them in relative order, completely by surprise. For one thing, there was no car in sight. Not to mention Sophia's face was bright red.

"You look like you've run a mile." It wasn't exactly the greeting Gina had rehearsed for the meeting. The plan had been a heartfelt *I'm sorry*, followed by... she hadn't decided. An offer to let Sophia pinch the skin on her upper arm and give it a good twist, maybe? It was the kind of thing that would've worked in kindergarten, which frankly had been the way Gina had behaved.

"Six and a half miles, actually." Huffing for breath, Sophia placed a leg on the lone picnic table bench outside the restaurant, stretching her calf. "I was trying for seven, but ran out of time and wanted a quick shower so I wasn't a complete mess. Sorry I'm late."

"Are you?" Gina wondered if her pounding heart gave her away. Sophia could probably hear it all the way where she was standing. "I hadn't noticed the time."

"I figured I better get some exercise in, given I'm about to blow my calorie allowance for the week." Sophia pointed to the 1950s trailer-type restaurant behind them. "Ready to stuff your face?"

It felt almost like a reprieve. It had been a full minute and somehow the topic of their fight hadn't come up at all. Stuffing their faces sounded way better than talking, but it left Gina confused. "I thought you were putting off the trip to Boo's until after you finished filming."

"That was before I realized the only cure for my crippling anxiety was a stress eating extravaganza. Something told me you might benefit from the same."

As Gina took in the wry expression on Sophia's face, a surge of hope passed through her. Could it have been her doom and gloom predictions about the nature of this meeting had been off the mark? Maybe *we have to talk* wasn't code for *I hate you* after all.

Gina let out a nervous laugh. "Was it the mental breakdown in my office the other day that gave me away?"

"It may have been a clue." Sophia chuckled, and

Gina relaxed a bit more. "I'm not saying a Boo's extra thick chocolate milkshake will fix everything. But I'm not saying it won't, either."

"I'm willing to give it a try."

They went inside and placed their order at the counter. Sophia had not been joking about her plan to consume a week's worth of calories, either. But it was when she remembered to order Gina's old-fashioned burger with no pickles, and then repeated the instructions to be sure the kid at the register understood, that Gina truly saw the light at the end of the dark tunnel they'd been stuck in the past few days and was relieved to discover it was not, in fact, an oncoming train.

When the order was totaled, Gina reached for her wallet, but Sophia placed a hand on Gina's arm. "I got it."

Considering her appalling behavior, Gina felt the least she could do was pay. From the tightness of Sophia's lips, Gina sensed this wasn't the hill to die on. Maybe Sophia was trying to be nice, or simply worried Gina was a poor academic who couldn't afford a burger on her own. Either way, Gina decided not to argue. "Thank you. I'll pay next time."

If there was a next time. For all Gina's sudden hopefulness, that very much remained to be seen.

"Should we eat outside?" Sophia asked, bouncing on the balls of her feet. "It's seventy-eight degrees today."

"With no wind. Your perfect temperature," Gina added, the memory from college popping into her head as clearly as if it had just happened.

Sophia tilted her head. "You remember that?"

"Of course. You joked about naming our future cat seventy-eight."

"I forgot about that." Sophia laughed.

The man dinged the bell, followed by him calling out, "Seventy-eight!"

"That's us!" Sophia exclaimed.

"Is that really our order number?" Not believing it, Gina peered over Sophia's shoulder, confirming the number. "Spooky."

"Or fate," Sophia countered, though Gina wasn't sure how to interpret it.

Sliding the overburdened yellow plastic tray onto the picnic table, Gina took a seat facing the street, giving Sophia the better view of the town common. "Are you sure you ordered enough?"

"I'm a nervous wreck. I want all the fries and onion rings. If you don't want your shake, I'll have it, too." Sophia proceeded to take a fry and dipped it into her shake.

Gina grimaced at what she had always deemed a thoroughly disgusting combination. "Either you have major PMS, or whatever you asked me here for today goes way beyond me groveling for forgiveness for acting like such an ass."

Sophia's eyes widened. "I had no expectation of you groveling, Gina. I hope you know that."

"Well, I'm sorry anyway," Gina rushed to say, not wanting any more time to pass without voicing the apology that was owed. "Now that I've choked *that* out, what's going on?"

Sophia popped the shake-covered fry into her mouth, chewing thoughtfully. "I'm not sure I know where to begin."

Gina's stomach flip-flopped. "That sounds ominous."

Sophia bobbed her head side to side, as if determining the severity of the news she was about to drop. "It's just—I thought I would have heard back about the script by now, and I haven't."

"I told you." Gina did her best to keep anything that could be construed as hurt or anger out of her tone, simply stating the facts as she saw them. "No one's going to want one of my scripts."

"That's not true." The passion of Sophia's argument came as a surprise. "I want it."

"Out of pity," Gina added, unable to keep back the comment.

"Will you stop!" Sophia ordered this with enough force Gina immediately snapped her mouth closed. Sophia dipped another fry into her shake. "I'm sorry I didn't ask first before sharing your work. That was wrong of me."

"I way overreacted," Gina admitted. "I was having a particularly bad day."

"I need you to know I did it for two reasons." Sophia bit into her lower lip, her nervousness palpable. Gina reminded herself not to bite Sophia's head off again, no matter what she said next. "I really do love the story."

After a pause, Gina prompted, "Is that one of the reasons or the windup?"

Sophia laughed, a sweet and spontaneous sound. "You see? That's what I like about you and your writing. I love your banter in real life, and it translated beautifully to your dialogue. I've read hundreds of scripts since moving to LA, and what you have is a real gift. But to answer your question, that was the first, and most important, reason."

"And the second…?" Gina waved for Sophia to fill in the blank before taking a massive bite of the juicy burger.

"I was afraid I was getting fired."

Gina swallowed before she finished chewing and choked. How had she not known things were this dire?

Sophia shoved the shake for Gina to drink, but it was the last thing she needed in the moment. She pounded on her chest in an effort of dislodging a lump of bun and beef from her throat.

Finally, Gina was able to wheeze out, "You were getting fired?"

"I told you before, the script Dix green lit was little

better than a soggy bag of manure, and it seems like IBC was already unhappy with him. Trying to hide the extent of Butch's injuries was the last straw. The bigwig himself, Ken Abrams, flew in from the west coast to let me know Dix was out."

"No second chances?" Considering the resources the network had sunk into the production, Gina was shocked, but Sophia shrugged, seeming to take it in stride.

"In this business, there rarely are. Ken brought a big-name producer with him whose company had just joined forces with IBC, and she took one look at the script and said what I'd been thinking all along. It was beyond salvaging. They were about to shut us down. That was when I remembered I still had your screenplay in my bag. I'd been reading it all morning, and I couldn't put it down. I'd planned to finish it after the meeting. Instead, I handed it over. The worst thing is, I don't know how it ends."

"They haven't called?"

Not answering, Sophia shoved an onion ring into her mouth.

"So, you're going to get fired, and it's my fault."

"It's not your fault! Stop taking all of my stuff onto your shoulders. You did it when you chivalrously broke up with me in college—which, by the way, is not a thing. And you're doing it now. You are not responsible for me. You're not responsible for Dr. Harlowe, for that matter. The only person you are responsible for is yourself." Sophia reached for Gina's hand, covering it with her own and holding Gina's gaze with her earnestly expressive eyes that sent a rush of every emotion known to humankind through Gina's soul all at once. "You need to start standing up for yourself."

"With you or Harlowe?"

"This isn't in my best interest to say but with everyone."

Gina looked away, watching a biker zip by on the rail trail. "You're right about Harlowe. He does still treat me like I'm his assistant, not an equal. The other day in my office after—" Her shrug implied their argument. "I started thinking of all the times he's dumped his administrative work onto me, always claiming he's so busy with the film. But, so am I." Gina sighed. "I just need to find a way to tell him how I feel."

"I really hope you do. But right now, I'd rather you tell me how you feel about, well, *me*."

Gina's brow furrowed. "What do you mean?"

"Before the incident in your office..." Sophia's eyes shifted toward the table, an uncertainty overtaking her. "I don't know. It seemed like we were... like we were getting back to how we used to be. When we were together. Maybe I'm mistaken, but—"

"No." Gina's response was as firm as it was quick. "You weren't mistaken. I felt it, too."

"All these years, I knew I missed you. But until I saw you again, I didn't know what a gaping hole your absence had been." Sophia looked up, her eyes watery.

"I like being around you. I can be myself with you, and in my line of work, that's rare. We're usually so rushed on sets, pretending to be happy when I'm miserable inside."

"I thought you liked your job."

"I do, and I don't. I mean, I'm lucky. I'm fulfilling my dream, but what they don't tell you is when you get the job you've always wanted, it's still a J-O-B." Sophia spelled the word, an endearing habit of hers Gina had forgotten, but when Sophia did it right then, it felt like being wrapped in a hug. "I really wish you had been honest with me back then."

"I know. I thought I was doing the right thing. The mature thing. I need you to understand how much it tore me apart." Gina took a breath, preparing to launch into the rest of her explanation, but Sophia shook her head.

"No, let me finish. I know why you did it, but do *you* know what part of it still makes me mad?"

Gina swallowed, shaking her head and feeling about an inch tall.

"You took away my agency. Whether to be with you or not was the single biggest decision of my life at that point—maybe it still is, even now—and I wasn't allowed to make it." Sophia flicked a tear away, sinking into silence.

"You're right," Gina answered, her voice breaking. "I was too young and stupid to realize it wasn't all about me."

"You martyred yourself, and I didn't even know it. I certainly didn't ask you to."

"It wasn't simply about me playing the martyr," Gina admitted, surprised at how much lighter she felt as the words tumbled out. "I didn't want to admit I wasn't good enough at the one thing I desperately wanted to do."

"You didn't trust me back then, but you need to now," Sophia urged. "Because you are good enough. You are."

"And yet"—Gina shook a fry at Sophia—"that hotshot producer from LA hasn't called."

"I haven't given up." Sophia grabbed the fry and popped it into her mouth with relish. "She's a fool if she passes on it, but she's just one producer. I know many. We'll keep hitting the pavement until we get it made."

"We?"

"It's really good, Gin. I want to make that film. I had high hopes about my future with IBC, but they're not the only game in town. I have a few connections."

"But—"

"No more buts. No more ifs. I'm the flipping Queen of Christmas, and I'm going to get this done if I have to start lopping off some heads to do it." A flush of excitement rose to Sophia's cheeks, and Gina found herself believing without a shred of doubt that this woman could and would do exactly as she said. "I've been miserable for ten years. I don't want to be anymore. So, I need to know. Do you feel the same?"

"Miserable? Yes." Gina gave her head an emphatic nod.

"Do you think we can have a second chance?"

The words slammed into Gina's chest. "Back in the day, you said second chances don't happen in real life."

"I said they hardly ever happen," Sophia argued. "There's a difference."

Gina's head swum. "I said horrible things…"

"Yeah. So did I." Sophia gave a *what can you do* shrug. "We still care deeply. If we didn't, we wouldn't have wasted the effort or agreed to talk. Yes, we've made mistakes, but I'm betting we're mature enough to make things work. That is if you want to."

Before Gina could answer, Sophia's phone buzzed, causing her to squeal. "It's Jill Davidson. She wants to meet tonight, with both of us."

"She…" Gina gasped as she made the connection. "*The* Jill Davidson? Producer of every major lesbian film in the past… like, *ever*?"

Sophia grinned, clapping her hands. "That's the one. Did I never get around to telling you that part?"

"No," Gina breathed. "And it's a good thing you didn't, or I would've died from nerves by now. Jill *freakin'* Davidson? Oh my God."

"So, what do you say?" Sophia's face was radiant with hope, making Gina's heart nearly burst.

"Yes." Gina vibrated from the top of her head all the way to the tips of her fingers and toes. "I say yes."

Sophia frowned slightly. "Is that a yes to dinner, or to, you know—"

"It's a yes to everything," Gina replied. "Anything and everything. If you're the one asking, I'm saying yes."

Sophia bounced in her seat, giggling. "Really?"

"Yes," Gina repeated. "See? Another yes. I would prove it to you right now once and for all by kissing you, but you have chocolate shake and French fry all over your mouth."

"I do?" Horrified, Sophia grabbed a napkin and wiped her face, laughing as the paper came away stained greasy brown. "Oh my God. I can't believe you didn't tell me before. Oh well. We'll make up for the kiss later. Right now, we need to get ready for dinner."

"Dinner?" Gina took in the mostly empty baskets and wrappers on the tray in front of them. In the intensity of their conversation, somehow, they'd managed to eat almost everything in sight.

"It's okay," Sophia assured her. "I'm an actor. I'll pretend to be hungry. Just follow my lead."

"Anywhere," Gina replied, happiness filling every space inside her not already occupied by burgers and fries.

CHAPTER FOURTEEN

"Do I look okay?" Sophia stepped into the cheery downstairs sitting room at the inn, holding her arms out from her body and swiveling at the waist from side to side so her long sundress swished around her ankles.

Perched on the love seat in the corner, Gina gazed at Sophia, a fire sparking in her eyes and growing more heated with each passing second. "You look stunning."

Sophia flushed, a current seeming to pass between them, until she had to look away to gather herself together before her body succumbed to spontaneous combustion. "Too stunning?"

Gina tilted her head to one side. "Is there such a thing?"

"You might be surprised. In my line of work there are so many pitfalls. Everything has to be perfectly coordinated or—" Sophia made a slicing motion across her throat. "I'm still paying in the tabloids for an ill-chosen white pantsuit I wore for a magazine photoshoot four years ago. I looked like a marshmallow."

"I bet you looked like an angel," Gina countered. "Anyone who said otherwise was jealous."

"I know everyone pokes fun at the people who wear nothing but black turtlenecks and jeans, but damn, I wish my life could be so simple." Sophia crossed to the other side of the small room, twirling in front of a full-length mirror that had been set up beside the fireplace. "Maybe I should change into the one with the tiny blue alligators?"

"No." Gina rose from the loveseat and moved to join Sophia, coming up behind her and wrapping her arms around Sophia's waist. "You look beautiful, and I like the peonies print."

"They're your favorite flower." Sophia sucked in her breath as Gina pressed her lips to Sophia's neck, just behind her right ear. She shuddered with delight, her head swimming in the delicious, musky scent that clung to Gina's skin.

"Peonies are a symbol of luck," Gina whispered into her ear. Sophia struggled to keep her focus, but it was a losing battle as desire swept over her. Gina could've been reciting her grocery list for all Sophia knew. The only thing she was aware of was the warm breath that tickled her hairline, threatening to bring Sophia to her knees. "We're going to need luck to get through dinner when all I want to do is slip into sweatpants, stretch out on the couch, and never move again."

Sophia giggled, thankful for the sudden dose of humor that turned the thermostat down on her desire to a more bearable level. Whatever else the evening had in store for Gina and her, they had an important meeting to get through first. "Mental note. Gorging on Boo's Burgers is not as wise an idea now as it was when we were twenty-two."

"I'm not sure it was all that smart then, either." Releasing Sophia's waist, Gina stepped back and lifted the loose shirt she'd changed into for dinner just enough to slip her thumb behind the waistband and give it a tug. The dark fabric yielded easily, stretching several inches. "Don't tell anyone, but it's elastic."

"Clever girl." Pressing at her full belly with a sigh, Sophia checked the clock on the mantel. "Is that time right?"

Gina consulted her watch. "No, it's five minutes slow."

"We have to go now!"

They dashed to Gina's car, which was parked outside the bed and breakfast, and were on the road in record time. Fortunately, Sholan Falls traffic didn't compare to LA's, and they arrived at Jill's hotel in the next town over five minutes early. The hotel had a restaurant attached, and it was there they were meeting with Jill to discuss Gina's script and the future of the film.

"I'm so glad you could make it," Jill said warmly, standing as the hostess led Sophia and Gina to her table. "I apologize for the short notice and for not getting in touch sooner. I was called to Atlanta to put out a fire on a film Sapphicsticated is doing down there, and it ended up being much more all-consuming than I'd anticipated."

"Not a problem at all," Sophia assured her, vowing not to let it show how terrified she'd been until the producer's text earlier that day.

"This must be Gina Mitchells, the screenwriter of the hour," Jill effused in a way that would have been over the top coming from most people but felt sincere from her.

"I'm not sure about that," Gina shuffled her feet, looking down at the carpet.

"I keep telling her how good the script is," Sophia told Jill, "but she doesn't believe me."

"The bane of being a writer. Never knowing what's good or not." Jill motioned for Sophia and Gina to be seated. "Sorry about making you drive all this way for dinner. I tried getting reservations in Sholan Falls, but the one place open for dinner was fully booked."

"Sean Henry's," Sophia said knowingly. It was the only restaurant in her hometown that offered a menu fancier than pub grub.

"That was the place. What was it like growing up in such a small town?" Jill asked as she flipped open her menu and perused the offerings.

"Quiet," Sophia said, opening her menu as well. She scanned the choices, looking for the smallest thing possible. "I forgot just *how* quiet until coming back. The other night I couldn't sleep, and I kept thinking the world must have ended because I didn't hear a thing. Not even a car. Just crickets."

A server approached the table. "Would you ladies like to start off with a drink?"

"Hell to the yes," Jill answered before Sophia had so much as processed the question. The producer seized the wine list and pointed out a bottle of Malbec with a questioning look. "Red okay? Let's do this one."

The man bobbed his head, turned on a heel, and headed toward the bar.

"Gina, I should start by saying how much I loved *Christmas at Rainbow Falls*," Jill gushed. "Speaking on behalf of International Broadcasting Conglomerate, I can tell you it has all the elements we're looking for in a holiday movie, along with some delightfully fresh twists."

Sophia leaned forward, unable to contain herself. "IBC wants to produce it?"

"Not only does IBC want it, they have authorized me to present a contract this evening," Jill confirmed, "but I, personally, would like to oversee this project as executive producer."

Sophia squealed, tapping her fingertips together. "This is a dream come true."

"You have my wife to thank for it," Jill said with a

laugh. "I shared it with Rhonda the other night, and she was in tears she loved it so much. What's more, I'm thrilled to say when I was in Atlanta, I dropped in on Hattie Dandrige. She's one hundred percent on board with taking on the role of the love interest, opposite your character, Sophia."

Sophia clasped her hands to her mouth, barely able to contain the type of yelp that would probably get them tossed out of this nice restaurant on their behinds. But how could she help it? Hattie Dandrige was one of the hottest young Black actors around.

"Did you say Hattie Dandrige?" Gina pressed a hand to her chest, as if she couldn't believe what she'd heard. Sophia's joy ebbed slightly as she wondered if her darling Gina was jealous. The truth was, Hattie Dandrige had nothing on Gina Mitchells, and Sophia would swear as much on a stack of Bibles daily if need be. Not that she intended to leave Gina with any doubts on the issue, just as soon as she could get her alone in her hotel room later tonight. It'd been a long day, on top of ten excruciating years.

"Yes." A flicker of concern crossed Jill's face. "That's not a problem, is it?"

The waiter returned, interrupting Gina's response with the presentation of the wine. He uncorked it with painstaking slowness, dashing some into a glass for Jill to taste. She simply waved for him to get on with it, while Gina stared as if unable to engage her vocal cords. Sophia's heart beat faster, uncertain what issue had her girlfriend so overcome.

Gina took a long sip of wine, and when she spoke, her voice sounded stilted. "It's just... I thought for sure... if you took the script..." She took another swallow of wine. "That you'd change the leads—"

"To a man and woman?" Jill guessed. "Not on my watch!"

"I'll admit before Sophia told me you were involved, that is what I thought." Gina chuckled. "It's just that these holiday movies are notoriously straight and white. I guess I assumed IBC wouldn't want to take on too many sacred cows in one go and would cast someone, well... white."

"Don't get me wrong, there *will* be some changes to the script." Jill circled the rim of her wine glass with a finger. "The biggest missing piece is the gazebo. Your script doesn't have a single scene set there, and after IBC built one for the town, there's no way we can't include it. But I would never allow someone to disrespect your story by changing something so integral to one of your main characters as her racial identity. You can rest easy about that."

Gina's lips flapped opened and then closed.

Sophia couldn't help but laugh. "You'll have to give her a second to process. You see, I only recently learned that Gina showed this same script to the Keynote Channel back in the day, and the feedback she received was much different."

"Oh?" Jill's brow furrowed. "I hope this won't be an issue. I assure you the offer I've brought is fair, but if there's a counter offer from Keynote, I'll need—"

"Counter offer?" Gina cut off Jill's sentence with a cackling laugh. "Hardly. Granted, this was ten years ago, but I was flat out told by their guy that no company would produce a holiday movie with female leads, period. And especially not one who was Black."

It was Jill's turn to be speechless before she muttered, "Fucking bastards."

"I'll drink to that!" Sophia hoisted her glass.

"I'm so tired of men, but that's neither here nor there." Jill reached for her briefcase, pulling out what appeared to be a contract. "Before we go any further, let me show you the deal we're prepared to offer."

Gina took the papers, her mouth falling open as she scanned the pages. Sophia was too far away to see the details, and Gina was apparently in too much shock to share them, but from the look of things, the offer was every bit as generous as Jill had hinted it would be.

"What do you think?" Gina started to speak, but Jill held up a hand. "I should be clear about one thing first. Given the tight filming schedule and the tweaks here and there to the script, we're going to need you to be hands-on. I understand you teach full-time, and I hear you're involved in planning the Comstock College Pride Festival, too. What I need to know is do you have the bandwidth to take this on? And don't bullshit a bullshitter."

"I wouldn't dare try," Gina said, shaking her head. She let out a breath, psyching herself up like a pitcher taking the mound. Finally, her head shake turned to a vehement nod. "Yes. I can do this. I may not sleep much, but there's no way I'm going to pass this up. Not after all of these years." Gina's eyes met Sophia's.

"Then, ladies, I can't tell you how happy I am to make this work. It's about time a script like this had its chance." Jill motioned to the server. "Can we get a bottle of champagne?"

"Wine *and* champagne?" Sophia was suddenly grateful that she had not arrived at this dinner with an empty belly.

"We're living it up!" Jill said with a laugh. "It's time to celebrate our victory over the cishet Christmas movie patriarchy!"

CHAPTER FIFTEEN

"What the...?" Gina craned her neck over the steering wheel, squinting at the chain-link fence that had definitely not stretched across this road earlier that night. She looked to Sophia in the passenger seat. "Now what do I do?"

Sophia's expression mirrored Gina's confusion as she eyed the unexpected blockade. "Make a left here."

Gina did as directed, almost immediately coming up against a cement barrier blocking the way, beyond which were several large storage trailers. "What's going on?"

"It has to be equipment for the shoot tomorrow," Sophia guessed. "See? That one is from an ice company. It takes a lot of effort to make it snow this time of year."

"I guess. Jill did say production would be off and running, but I didn't expect all of downtown Sholan

Falls to be closed off in a matter of hours." Gina carefully reversed the car back onto the main road, sighing as she contemplated her options. "I can almost see the inn from here, but the only way I can think to get there is to head back the way we came and take the highway down to the next exit."

"That'll take us thirty minutes out of the way or longer," Sophia said. "Also, it's under construction until the fall and down to one lane of traffic overnight."

Gina let out a frustrated growl. "Oh, for fuck's sake. We could park in the municipal lot by the library and walk back there in less time."

"Yes. Let's do that." Sophia sounded relieved.

"What?"

"It's a beautiful night, and a walk across the common would be romantic. Besides, the sooner we get back to my hotel..." Her voice trailed off in a way that offered so much promise, Gina wasn't about to argue.

Fortunately, all of the roads leading to the parking lot were unobstructed, and Gina easily located a space. "I won't get towed, will I? If I park overnight, that is."

"What do you mean by *if*?" Sophia pretended to pout as she got out of the car. "Did you have other plans for this evening? A hot date, maybe?"

"Oh, I'm definitely hoping for a hot date," Gina teased as she closed the car door and locked it.

"In that case, follow me." Sophia took Gina by the

hand, sending a burning wave of anticipation through her.

They made it to the edge of the common only to realize that even walking had its impediments this evening. A security guard in a golf cart blocked the only opening in the temporary barrier that had been erected by the film crew a few weeks before.

"I thought this was kept open unless it was a hot set," Gina commented in a low voice. The security guard appeared to be engrossed in his phone and didn't look up as they approached.

"It must be because of all the extra snow making equipment. It costs a fortune, so they probably needed to up the security for insurance purposes." Sophia raised her hand in greeting as she called out, "Todd? Is that you?"

The security guard looked up from his phone and smiled. "Evening, Ms. Rossi."

"We're trying to get to the other side of the common," Sophia explained, employing her most charming tone. "Would it be okay if we cut across?"

"It's supposed to be cast and crew only—" Todd started to say, but Sophia jumped in before he could finish.

"Perfect! This is Gina Mitchells, the new screenwriter."

Todd nodded, seeming satisfied by the explanation and all around a little bored. "Okey doke. Go on through."

"Thanks!" Sophia led Gina through the narrow space between the golf cart and the barrier. By the time they'd passed, the guard was already lost in his phone screen.

When they'd walked about halfway across the common, Sophia stopped and stared upward into the inky black sky. "Do you hear that?"

Gina slanted her head to hear better, but all she could make out was the hum of crickets. "What?"

"Exactly." Sophia squeezed Gina's fingers. "It's so quiet."

"It's after midnight." Gina tried suppressing a yawn.

"Don't you dare be getting tired on me," Sophia scolded. "We still have plans for tonight."

"Oh, do we?" Gina gave her eyebrows a suggestive wiggle as her fatigue evaporated.

"Yes. But first, I want to check out the gazebo." Sophia took Gina by the hand, leading her across a section of lawn that was slightly mushy from rain earlier in the night.

"Tonight?" Despite the question, Gina trotted along beside Sophia. She'd learned years ago there was no use arguing when the woman got an idea in her head.

"Yes, tonight. You have to add it to your script, remember?" Sophia climbed the three wooden steps, pulling Gina into the gazebo behind her.

"I don't think Jill meant I had to do it before morning." Gina spun in a slow circle, taking in not only the gazebo but the whole stretch of downtown that was decorated like a Christmas fantasy. It all felt unreal. "I still can't believe IBC bought my script."

"I can," Sophia answered, wrapping her arms around Gina and pulling her close to her chest. "You better start believing it, too, because you have to be on set in about five hours."

"Maybe we should sleep here for the night." Gina laughed at her own joke, but instead of joining in, Sophia eyed her with a look Gina hadn't seen in years, except in her dreams. She knew what it meant but couldn't stop herself from asking, "Why are you staring at me like that?"

"Like what?" Sophia inched closer, nibbling on her bottom lip in a way that somehow managed to come across as innocent and suggestive at the same time.

Gina raised her eyebrows, not buying the innocent act one bit. "It's coming across a little lecherous."

"Only a little?" Sophia's voice was low and sultry, and her pupils tripled in size.

Gina's body sank into the feel of Sophia's arms around her, their lips only an inch or two apart. Even that distance was way too much. Gina couldn't stand it any longer, like the years of not being able to kiss Sophia were hitting her all at once.

Sophia must have felt the same because the next moment she grabbed Gina's shirt, balling it in both hands as she pulled her the last few inches, kissing

Gina like they'd never kissed before. It was entirely unique, yet felt like the most natural thing in the world. Both of them deepened the connection simultaneously, pulling the other closer, getting entangled, but not caring.

The only thing that mattered was that they were back together.

"I've missed this," Gina panted as she finally freed her lips long enough to mumble a few words.

"I've missed everything." The way Sophia moaned the last words was a pretty big clue what *everything* entailed.

Desire roared to life within her, burning the deepest, unseen reaches of Gina's being. "Nice gazebo, but should we head back to your room?"

Sophia shook her head, slowly and with such purpose Gina was taken aback. A moment later Sophia reached for the front of Gina's shirt, unbuttoning it. Her lips fluttered across Gina's jaw, down her neck, and even further down her chest.

"Someone will see us." Even as Gina scouted the common for signs of trespassers, she made no attempt to escape Sophia's grasp, or to stop her from easing yet another button from its hole.

"No one's up," Sophia mumbled into the crevice between Gina's breasts. "The security guard is the only person around for a mile."

"What if he's a Peeping Tom?" Running her fingers through Sophia's hair, Gina couldn't decide what would be worse. Having to wait another second for Sophia's touch or having a security guard in a golf cart see it happen.

"His name's Todd. Tom is my future brother-in-law," Sophia joked.

"What if he's a Peeping Todd, then?" Gina snorted at her own ridiculousness, even as she turned into a puddle at every kiss and caress Sophia sent her way without any intention of stopping her.

With a subtle flick, Gina's bra cup slipped beneath her breast. Sophia's tongue flicked across Gina's exposed nipple, fast and wet, even as she moved her hand down Gina's stomach, sliding it beneath her waistband with ease. She pulled Gina's nipple into her mouth with a hard suck and then released it slowly as the nipple stretched taut.

A finger breeched the elastic waistband of Gina's underwear, showing no signs of stopping there.

"Uh—" Gina was about to say something to the effect of perhaps they should cool it and get to the room when her back met with the hard post of the gazebo's railing. A second later, the heat of Sophia's hand cupping her sex chased all thoughts from Gina's head but one.

More.

The flavor of Sophia's kisses still lingering on her lips, Gina grasped the back of Sophia's head to claim her mouth again with a fierceness that would've surprised her if she'd been thinking at all. But who could spare the energy for thought when it took all Gina had to feel what she was feeling and not fly apart?

As their tongues battled for position, Sophia traced the tip of her thumb along the wetness of Gina's slit, teasing the folds open. She stroked Gina's clit slowly then faster.

Gina drew a hissing breath as Sophia's finger slid inside, while a thumb continued to circle Gina's engorged bud. A hot searing bolt of pleasure coursed through her as a second finger joined the first. Gina felt every inch of Sophia's fingers working inside her, bringing her closer to the moment of release.

"You still worried someone might see?" Sophia whispered.

Gina angled her hips to allow Sophia even more access, stifling a cry as the woman pressed into the spot guaranteed to drive her mad. "Huh?"

"Never mind." Sophia giggled. "I think I know the answer."

The laughter awoke a spark of joy in Gina's breast, a feeling that had been absent from her life for so long it nearly took her breath away. She let out a cry, her eyes growing wide as the fear of discovery belatedly poked her brain.

"Shh. It's okay." Instead of pulling back, Sophia increased her efforts. Gina's body tightened around Sophia's fingers. "You're almost there. I can tell."

"I can't believe… I'm…" Gina felt warm all over, an

odd, giddy rush vibrating through her like a guitar string being plucked. She came hard, holding onto Sophia so as not to collapse into a puddle.

"This is the one thing every holiday movie is missing." Sophia gave one final thrust before allowing her fingers to slip out. "A beautiful, hot sex scene."

"In… a… gazebo," Gina managed to say between sharp breaths.

"Precisely." Sophia repositioned Gina's bra and carefully fastened the shirt buttons while Gina pulled herself together. "And no Peeping Todd."

"You're sure?" Gina asked, belated fear of being caught having sex in an open-air gazebo in the middle of the night jolting her.

Sophia nodded in the direction from which they'd come. The golf cart was still in the same place, and even from a distance, Gina could tell the occupant was slumped to one side, probably fast asleep.

"See? Completely undetected." Sophia flashed a bright smile, pairing it with a naughty wink. "Now, let's get back to the hotel room."

"Not so fast." Gina's mind now put at ease that they were not in any danger of getting caught, Gina decided it was time to flip the script on her impish vixen. Wrapping an arm around Sophia's waist, Gina twirled her until they'd switched places, with Sophia's back now firmly against the post. "I suggest you hold onto the railings."

"Why?" A hint of nervousness rang out in Sophia's laugh. "What are you planning to do?"

Gina answered by dropping to her knees, grateful the floor of the gazebo was soft pine and not something unpleasant like gravel. Not that it would've stopped her. Her body might feel differently about it in the morning, but for right now, Gina felt invincible.

Putting one hand on each of Sophia's legs, Gina lifted the hem of the floral sundress, inching it along Sophia's thighs until it was just above Gina's head. Gina pulled the fabric over her hair, letting it fall behind her like a veil.

"Gina!" Sophia chided, although it was only her words that protested. As Gina shifted Sophia's panties to one side, it did not escape her notice that Sophia widened her stance to give better access.

The scent of Sophia's arousal catapulted Gina back in time, reliving all the many hours and days she'd spent buried between Sophia's thighs. Not wanting to waste another second, Gina took Sophia into her mouth, devouring her. The sweet taste of her juice caressed Gina's tongue. It was intoxicating, and she never wanted to stop.

Gina licked with long, sure strokes, entering Sophia with her tongue before adding first one finger and then another.

Sophia's hands clutched the railing. Her low, deep moans spurred Gina to continue.

Gina could hardly believe this was happening. Was

she really making love to the one woman she'd desired and adored more than anyone in her life, in a gazebo in the middle of the town common?

Impossible!

Yet, after the evening she'd had, with all of her dreams coming true, this seemed such a natural and fitting conclusion. How could the perfect day end in any other way?

And, fuck, Gina had missed the way Sophia tasted, her musky scent, and the tiny pants she made the closer she came to bliss. The pants turned more rugged, and Gina sensed Sophia was struggling to stay on her feet. Gina focused all her energy on getting Sophia to come. It was the best way to end the evening.

No, it was the best way for their second act. Together.

Sophia's legs trembled, and she clawed Gina's head, without actually touching her since her head was under the sundress. There was a dramatic shudder, and then Sophia's legs nearly buckled, and Gina had to act fast to get to her feet to keep Sophia on hers.

"Now should we head back to the inn?" Gina asked.

Sophia opened her eyes, wearing the expression of a drunken sailor who had yet to gain her sea legs. "Give me time to recover enough so I can walk."

Gina chuckled, feeling pretty damned proud of

herself, too. "Do you think this would work for incorporating the gazebo into the script?"

"You'd better be joking." Sophia made a weak attempt to make herself presentable, though it was a delightfully lost cause. "I'm not sure I'll ever be able to look at a gazebo the same way again."

"I should hope not." Gina held out her arm for Sophia to take. "Come on. Let's head back before we get caught. I'd like to run this scene again a couple times back in the room, just to see if we can make some improvements."

CHAPTER SIXTEEN

In the glow of a dim reading lamp on the hotel nightstand, Sophia traced the curve of Gina's cheek with the tip of her finger. She started with the lightness of a feather, gradually increasing the pressure so as to rouse the sleeping woman as gently as possible.

"Hmmm…" was all Gina seemed able to say. It was clear she wasn't fully awake, but even so, she wore the most beautiful smile Sophia had ever seen.

After two weeks of waking up together every morning, Sophia was beginning to recall that Gina had never been the most coherent or talkative at the start of the day. It was a trait they'd once shared, before years of early call times had turned Sophia, however begrudgingly, into at least a semi-morning person.

"Hmmm, to you, too." Sophia snuggled closer, placing her head on Gina's breast, which was bare, along with the rest of her. That had been a definite perk of reuniting in full-blown adulthood. Without roommates to worry about, both Gina and Sophia felt free to indulge in being naked as much as they pleased.

And, they had. A lot.

"Hmmm?" Gina responded to Sophia's imitation of her in exaggerated fashion, cracking one eye open to see how her joke landed. "It's a good thing I'm the writer."

"Are you suggesting I'm not good at dialogue?" Sophia demanded with mock outrage.

"Delivering it? Pure perfection."

Sophia rolled on top of Gina's delightfully soft naked body, using one knee to separate her legs. "Pretty sure I'm good at delivering a lot more than lines."

The spark of desire in Gina's eyes was impossible to miss, but even so, she turned her mouth away when Sophia came in for a kiss, offering her cheek instead.

"Hey!" Sophia protested.

"We have to work," Gina replied with obvious regret. "If we start kissing, we may never make it to the set."

"We have a few minutes," Sophia playfully pouted. "It's not my fault you slept in."

"Slept in?" Gina shot a withering look at the dark window to one side of her. "It's not even light out yet."

"Doesn't mean the work day hasn't started." Sophia couldn't quite suppress a sigh as she thought of all the predawn call times she'd been saddled with over the years. "This is the glamorous part of making movies you've been missing."

"Can't say as I've *missed* it. But you know what I do regret?" Apparently willing to tempt herself into breaking her own resolve, Gina traced Sophia's spine with both hands, not stopping until she cupped her ass.

"All the terrible bad coffee and stale donuts you didn't get?" Sophia nipped at Gina's earlobe before nuzzling the crook of her neck.

Gina squirmed but in the good way. "Not being by your side. These last two weeks have been amazing, haven't they?"

"We agree on that topic." Sophia wanted to stay in bed all day, but knew that wasn't possible. Even so, she couldn't resist asking, "You sure I can't talk you into a quickie?"

"You probably could," Gina admitted. "But you shouldn't. I have to head straight to campus after going over the script with Jill this morning. I can't teach a class with you all over my face."

"Why not?" Sophia offered her most impish grin.

Gina wriggled with more intensity this time, causing Sophia to roll to one side enough to allow for an escape. "Shower. Now!"

Propping herself up on one elbow, Sophia pulled out her biggest weapon, the batting of her long eyelashes. "You aren't the boss of me."

"Technically, as one of the producers, aren't you the boss of me?" Lifting the covers off herself, Gina made a quick exit from the bed.

"I'll compromise," Sophia offered, trying to think of any way to keep Gina from completing her escape. "Shower sex!"

"You like naming sex. You've been talking about gazebo sex for two weeks, and now I guess it's going to be shower sex." Gina rummaged through a pile of discarded clothing, pulling out a bathrobe from amidst the clutter and throwing it over her shoulders.

"Sometimes you complain about the oddest things." Sophia rose to her feet, jutting out a naked hip by way of showcasing everything Gina was arguing against. "You *sure* I can't change your mind about the shower?"

"You're totally cheating!" The glint in Gina's eyes told Sophia she'd won the argument.

"Come on. I'll even help you scrub your back." Sophia took Gina's hands in hers and began leading her toward the bathroom. "It'll go faster that way, and I wouldn't want you to be late."

By the time they arrived on the set—with ten minutes to spare, which Sophia considered a personal achievement—everyone was moving to and fro, frantically getting everything ready for the day. They would be shooting outdoors at a simulated holiday fair, ending with the big tree lighting scene. In Sophia's experience, both were vital elements of a successful film, but she had a renewed sense of excitement at experiencing them in her hometown.

The moment Sophia and Gina strode onto the set, Jill made a beeline for Gina.

"There you are! I have a question about these lines I've circled." The producer handed over a coffee-stained script. No sooner had she done this than her attention was caught by the crew that was busy wrapping pine boughs around a lamppost. "Oh! They've got the wrong garland. I'll be right back."

Sophia gave Gina a quizzical look, but Gina was too busy reading the page, reaching into her bag for a pen. Sophia chuckled to herself. It had only taken Gina a few days to become as accustomed to the controlled mayhem of a Christmas movie set as Sophia was.

With the garland error rectified, Jill returned with a plate of cannoli. "Sophia, I both love and hate your mother. If she keeps bringing these over, I'm going to need a whole new wardrobe. Who knew cannoli was the perfect breakfast?"

"Is that what this smudge is, here?" Gina pointed to a splotch of something on the script in her hand. "Cannoli guts?"

"It's called cannoli *filling*, word genius," Sophia mocked, giving Gina a good-natured shoulder bump.

"Are they fresh?" Gina asked, paying no attention to Sophia.

"Definitely. Mrs. Rossi was here before me this morning, which is saying something." Jill chomped into the cannoli, getting the filling on her chin, which she wiped with the back of her hand.

"I don't know who's more excited about being on set: my mother, Gina, or maybe Peeping Todd." Sophia waggled her brows at Gina, getting back at her for not laughing at the word genius joke, even if it hadn't been overly witty.

"Who's Peeping Todd? Do I need to speak to security?" Jill glanced around suspiciously, as if expecting to find a man in a trench coat hiding behind the nearest bush.

"He *is* security," Sophia said with a snicker.

"It's a long story," Gina added, gnashing her teeth at Sophia.

"Speaking of stories," Jill said, "that reminds me. Your interview is up on *The Rising Celesbian* blog."

"Already?" Gina sipped her coffee, staring longingly at the cannoli Jill was polishing off. Sophia made a mental note to ask her mom for half a dozen next time they dropped by for a visit.

"Yep, and I've lined up some morning show interviews for you and Sophia," Jill added, "after we finish shooting."

"At least now we don't have to worry about people finding out we're dating," Sophia said to Gina.

"Quite the contrary," Jill assured them. "I want you two to talk it up. How the Pride Parade brought you two together. Oh, there'll be television crews at Pride as well. I really hope you two aren't keeping any other secrets because we're going to have cameras on you until the movie comes out."

As Jill chuckled, Sophia studied Gina's face. Not that it was a secret, exactly, but there was the small issue that Gina hadn't been entirely forthcoming with Comstock College—which was to say, her boss, in particular—about this side gig. Sophia was amazed at how cool Gina managed to play it, all things considered.

While Gina hadn't missed teaching a single class, and she'd been putting in as many hours on the documentary promo as before, Sophia had a feeling Professor Harlowe wouldn't like Gina wasting time on a Christmas movie. *Crap for Neanderthals,* she seemed to recall the man calling such forms of entertainment when she'd been a student in one of his classes. From everything Gina had said, Sophia didn't think the years had softened the prig.

"I really should get in the makeup chair," Sophia said.

"I still need to go over today's script before I head to campus, and I'm running late."

"I thought you had a few hours."

"I got a quote-unquote *urgent* text earlier from Harlowe." Gina gave a slight eye roll, the only fitting response to the way her boss tended to elevate his own needs above everything else. "He wants to talk to me about something."

"He didn't say what?"

"You know how he is. I told him I could drop in before class, although I think I might have to postpone until after, depending on how long the revisions take with Jill." Gina gave Sophia a kiss on the cheek. "See you later tonight."

"You'll be here for the tree lighting scene?"

Gina grinned. "Wouldn't miss it."

Sophia had made it about halfway to the makeup trailer when she was stopped in her tracks as her mom and sisters swarmed around her. "What are you guys doing here?"

"We're extras for the tree lighting," her mom stated as if that should have been obvious.

Sophia blinked. "That's not for hours. It's not even dark out yet."

"I want to be ready for my closeup." Her mom pressed her hands together, exuding glee. "From what the director told us at the audition, we have to pretend like we're watching the tree at Rockefeller Center."

"Something like that," Sophia confirmed.

Her mom wrinkled her nose as she took in the artificial tree that had been erected near the gazebo. "It's not that impressive of a tree. The real one the town puts up over the holidays is way nicer."

"Yes, well it's May," Sophia pointed out. "And starting to get hot. A real tree now would dry out and burst into flames. By the time the scene makes it through post-production, it'll look like a million bucks. That's why it's called acting."

"What kind of award will I be up for?"

"What are you talking about?" Bella demanded, making a face as she rubbed her swollen belly.

"How are you feeling?" Sophia asked her sister.

"Best Supporting Actor?" Sophia's mom continued, paying no attention to her older daughter.

"The baby's been kicking, but I'm fine," Bella replied.

"I have ten bucks that her water breaks during filming tonight." Carrie seemed way too jolly about the thought.

"She's not due for weeks," their mom corrected, turning her focus back to Sophia. "At the Oscar's."

"What are you—Hold on a second." Sophia choked back a laugh. "Do you think being an extra in a TV movie will earn you an Academy Award nomination? I've starred in twenty of these things, and I've never even been nominated for a Golden Globe."

"You don't have my joyful face down." As if to bolster her claim, she showed Sophia her Rockefeller Center expression again. The three sisters exchanged *Mom's gone crazy* glances, but it was clear none of the Rossi girls wanted to burst her bubble.

"I guess we'll see," Sophia said, sucking in her cheeks. She was trying to keep from laughing, but it quickly became unnecessary as Sophia spied a familiar face that sapped her of any desire to laugh. "Is that Evan Harlowe?"

Her mom and sisters offered little more than

confused faces, but there was no doubt about it. The professor was heading right for Gina, with Peeping Todd giving chase. Sadly, not in his golf cart, because Sophia realized with surprising intensity how much she would have liked to see the snobby professor mowed down to size.

Without wasting a second, Sophia began running toward Gina, waving her arms for attention. But it was no use. Gina and Jill were still buried in the script. It was only when the professor was a few yards away that Gina glanced up. Her horror-filled eyes making it clear whatever was about to happen wasn't going to be good.

"Professor Harlowe?" Gina began. "I was planning to meet with you—"

"Don't give me that," he all but yelled, looking mad enough to bite Gina's head off and use it like a doggie chew toy. "What the hell do you think you're doing?"

CHAPTER SEVENTEEN

Gina took a step back, flinching as she did. For one brief but shocking moment, she was convinced Dr. Harlowe was about to throw a punch. His eyes seemed crazed, his seething anger completely at odds with the festive holiday decor surrounding them. A few members of the crew looked on in stunned silence, as if they, too, didn't know what to make of this scene.

"I'm sorry," she stammered, "but I have no idea—"

"Sir, you can't be here." As the security guard made a brave lunge to grab the professor's arm, Gina vowed never to refer to him as Peeping Todd again.

"Do you know who I am?" Harlowe growled. "Let go of me."

"It's okay, Todd. He's..." Gina's explanation died on her lips. She wasn't sure what to say. While he was the head of her department at the college, as long as she was working on the film set, the professor wasn't technically her boss. Not here.

"Are you sure you'll be okay?" Todd pressed. By this point, Sophia had come up, too, her expression mirroring the security guard's concern.

Gina nodded to both of them, forcing herself to pull it together despite feeling shaky inside. She leveled her gaze at Professor Harlowe, not sure she'd ever seen him so enraged. "Is there an emergency that you needed to track me down when I was heading to campus momentarily?"

"Yes, I'd say there is." Harlowe's voice boomed, prompting Gina to wave her hands at him to turn it down. More crew members were staring, and Gina's initial feeling of shock was morphing into profound embarrassment.

"Why don't you go to my trailer to talk in private?" Sophia suggested, coming to Gina's rescue.

But instead of agreeing like a rational human, the professor's eyes sparked with renewed ire. "You. I should've known you'd turn back up like a bad penny."

"What does that mean?" Sophia demanded, but the man had refocused on Gina.

"I hope you know you've ruined any chance of ever making tenure. Do you really think the committee will be impressed by this Christmas film?" The way he said *Christmas* with such derision, he might as well have been accusing Gina of making pornography.

Sophia took a step forward, giving Gina heart palpitations as she imagined her girlfriend challenging Harlowe to an actual fistfight. "A major entertainment company is producing a movie Gina wrote the script for. Why wouldn't the committee be impressed?"

"This isn't a movie." Harlowe's lip curled in a way Gina had never seen. She'd heard the rumors he could be condescending and nasty, but until this moment, she'd never witnessed it firsthand. Impatient, yes, especially when they had a tight deadline. But this was something meaner spirited. Hurtful, even. "These pathetic stories are nothing but catnip for idiots."

"I think that's enough," Gina said, her voice steady and firm, speaking to her mentor like she might have to with the kids on the festival committee when their bickering got out of control. "I assume you came here for a reason."

Something other than bashing her and Sophia—hell, the entire Christmas movie industry—in their own workplace. The more Gina processed it, the more she realized Dr. Harlowe was completely out of line.

"You don't think I have a legitimate interest in what you put your name to? Your name is tied to mine, don't forget." Harlowe let out a loud breath, clearly exasperated but making a belated attempt to rein it in. "More importantly, you do not have time for this nonsense. There are three interviews that need to be augmented. Audio should suffice." Harlowe handed over a folder. "All the details are in here."

Gina flipped through the file with mounting confusion. "All of these have already been edited. We can't touch them without adding an extra week of work, at least."

"Like I said, you don't have time to waste." That mean expression took over the professor's features again, like an alien taking possession. "You know, Gina. If you'd done your job right the first time, they wouldn't have to be redone."

"I can..." Gina caught herself before she did what she usually would in these circumstances, apologize and agree to try harder. Maybe it was his expression that made the words sink in, or maybe she'd finally reached her breaking point. Either way, she found herself saying, "You've been doing the interviews, Evan. Not me."

Gina stifled a gasp. Had she just called him by his first name? She'd never done that before that she could recall, and especially not with such anger in her tone.

It did not go unnoticed.

"Why *this* movie?" Harlowe's tone and expression grew accusatory as he motioned to the staff moving a Christmas tree from the candy shop to the cafe next door for the next scene, the tree looking slightly worse for wear. "This is going to ruin you. You might as well have tried out to be a cheerleader for the Patriots. That's just as bad—no, this is worse. This is going on your IMDb page, right next to our films. No one is going to take you seriously anymore. Or me."

Which, it was becoming increasingly clear, was really what this was all about. Harlowe didn't care about Gina at all. He was only concerned for his own reputation. Paranoid, more like.

In her most calming way, Gina attempted to smooth his ruffled feathers. "I really don't think—"

"Clearly not." Harlowe's face grew flushed, and it was obvious her attempt to calm him had had the opposite effect. "I'll call the tenure committee, but I'm going to have to be honest with them. You've messed up my documentary while chasing this stupid dream of yours. I truly thought I'd beaten that out of your head before you graduated, but I guess I was wrong."

Gina stood speechless, trying and failing to recall a time she'd ever shared her dream of screenwriting with Harlowe, let alone him attempting to beat it out of her, as he'd said. Why would he think he'd had anything to do with it all those years ago?

"If you know what's best for you, quit this right now and come back to campus with me." As Harlowe spun around to leave, Sophia broke her long silence.

"Hey, a—Professor Harlowe." Sophia's jaw was tight, as she stopped herself from calling him an asshat, a sure sign she was in fighting mode. Gina felt her spirits plummet as he wheeled back around, eyes shooting daggers at her girlfriend. "I know you don't get this, but Gina is a professor. Not a teacher's assistant. Not a grad student. She's your equal. No, I'd say she's far superior to you. And, her screenplay is the best I've ever read."

"Sophia," Gina hissed, her stomach roiling. Why was the woman insisting on poking an angry bear?

"It's true," Sophia said in her defense.

Harlowe blinked twice at Sophia's outburst, then turned from her like she was nothing more than a gnat buzzing around his face.

"I thought you were better than this, Gina. I really did, or I wouldn't have... If you don't fix the interviews, consider yourself fired from the project. And don't think I can't do it." At this point, he turned to Sophia, venom seeping into his words. "Don't think I can't, Little Miss Christmas. When it comes to the Comstock College Film Studies department, I am in charge. Hell, I'm basically God."

With that, Dr. Harlowe strode away with such exaggerated determination he looked like a diva flouncing off a stage. Despite the seriousness of what had transpired, Gina nearly burst out laughing, especially because he had to walk all the way across the green lawn and started to lose steam halfway.

"Did Professor Harlowe just threaten me?" Gina mused when he was gone. The entire interaction hardly seemed real. "He said he would talk to the tenure committee, but was that to help my case or to sink it?"

"My money's on sinking it," Sophia said, her

expression grim. "I think he dumped his entire workload on you, too. Again."

Feeling off balance, Gina reached out for Sophia's shoulder to steady herself. "I don't know what to think. This can't be happening."

Sophia placed an arm around Gina's waist. "Sadly, that was all too real."

Gina opened the folder Harlowe had handed her, letting out a moan as she skimmed the page. "How am I supposed to get all this done?"

"I can help."

Gina shut her eyes. "What's the point? If he torpedoes my tenure application, I might as well quit."

"Over the years," Sophia said in her sternest troop-rallying tone, "I've dealt with a lot of people like Evan Harlowe, and do you know why they act so almighty and powerful?"

"Because they are?"

"No, because they aren't, and they can't handle it." Sophia shifted, taking both Gina's hands in hers and looking her in the eyes. "You are young and talented. The whole world is your future."

"But without Professor Harlowe—"

"Without him, what?" Sophia squeezed Gina's hands. "He needs you. That much is clear. For all he wants you to think he has the power, he needs you. If he didn't, he wouldn't be so angry."

"But I didn't tell him about this film, and I did commit to a portion of the documentary being ready to present at the Pride Festival." A million other reasons the professor's behavior was justified crowded into Gina's mind, but before she could give them voice, Sophia shook her head.

"Don't start that again. You're always defending him. Does he tell you every project he does in his free time?"

"Well, no," Gina admitted.

"And does your contract with the college require you to share that information with him?"

"No."

"What exactly did you do wrong then?"

"Nothing, I guess…"

"Exactly." Another squeeze of the hands, harder this time. "Nothing. You've done nothing since I got here except work your ass off covering for that man's laziness. You grade his papers. You redo his work. You're doing everything for this documentary, and he's taking all the credit."

"I'm being listed as the co-director," Gina argued.

"While he's listed as a director *and* the producer. It's not right."

Gina's shoulders slumped. "Maybe not, but I won't be listed at all if I don't get these interviews redone. I'm afraid I'll have to work all weekend."

"And miss Mom's cookout on Sunday?" Sophia looked horrified. "Absolutely not. I told you I'll help. You just tell me what to do. Okay?"

For the first time since Professor Harlowe had

burst onto the set, Gina found herself able to smile. The encounter had left her on edge, dredging up serious doubts about her working relationship with a mentor she once thought she'd understood. They were doubts she'd pushed aside for far too long, lacking the strength or mental energy to address them.

"Okay." Gina's heart swelled. Something about Sophia being willing to fight alongside her gave Gina the confidence she needed. "Thank you."

CHAPTER EIGHTEEN

"Are you sure you don't mind making these calls?" Standing in the room at the bed and breakfast on Saturday morning, Gina patted her pockets, having once again misplaced her keys.

"You're the epitome of the absent-minded professor." Sophia dropped Gina's keys into her open palm. "And, no. I'll be fine. You have enough on your plate driving to Connecticut to complete the missing interview."

"Last time I checked, your plate is just as full," Gina argued.

Sophia blew a puff of breath upward, shifting the hair from in front of her eyes. "Will you just trust me? I can handle doing some simple fact-checking."

After sending Gina out the door with a kiss, Sophia set to work on her mission. She hadn't wanted Gina to know, but Sophia had an ulterior motive for helping. As

Gina had flipped through the file the day before on the set, Sophia had recognized one of the names on the list.

Larry Jacobs.

He'd been an executive at the Keystone Channel when she'd made her first film. More importantly, and something she doubted Gina knew, he was married to Alex Cross, the man who'd once convinced Gina to abandon all hope of a career as a screenwriter. Seeing Larry's name on this list had come as a shock, as she'd been unaware of a connection between either Larry or Alex and Professor Harlowe. She suspected there was obviously more to this story than met the eye, and Sophia intended to find out what.

After downing an extra strong cup of coffee, Sophia sat at the desk and fired up her laptop. The video meeting had already been confirmed, so all she had to do was click to begin. Soon, the image of a man with a salt and pepper beard filled the screen.

"Sophia Rossi." Larry grinned. "What a sight for sore eyes you are after all these years. You haven't changed a bit."

"I see you're still a flatterer, Larry," Sophia teased, feeling her face flush. His charm was hard to resist, which she suspected was the whole point of it. The man had made a career working with actors, after all, a group famously well-known for lapping up praise like kittens drinking milk.

"I'll admit to being a little confused. Not that I'm

not delighted to be talking to you, but that Harlowe fellow said I'd be speaking to his assistant. A Gina someone, I think it was."

Assistant, was it? Sophia struggled to keep her anger in check. It figured Harlowe would present Gina in that way.

"Honestly?" Sophia's belly tightened as she prepared to tell the truth of why she was calling. "While I do have a few questions to clarify for the documentary, it's Alex I was hoping to speak to."

"Alex?" Larry's face clouded. "He wants nothing to do with this project, or anything Evan Harlowe has a hand in."

Interesting. And yet, Larry had agreed to be interviewed on camera for it. Why?

"It's nothing to do with the film. I promise," Sophia said with caution. "It's more a personal matter."

Larry's brow furrowed, but after a moment of silence, he turned and called to someone off camera. "Honey? Do you have a minute? It's Sophia Rossi for you."

"Sophia Rossi?" she heard a man's voice say, clearly bewildered. "What would she want with me?"

"Tell him it's about my girlfriend, Gina," Sophia urged. "Gina Mitchells."

Before Larry had the chance to relay the message, Alex appeared on the screen. "Okay, Larry-bear. I'll take it from here. Why don't you take the dogs down for their walk?"

Larry gave him a questioning look. "You don't want me to stay on the call?"

"Nah. This won't take long, and the boys are getting restless." Even as he said it, Sophia heard barking in the background. With a nod, Larry headed off camera. Alex didn't speak again until after Sophia heard a door close or so she conjured up in her mind. At that point, Alex puffed out his cheek, letting the air slowly seep out as he seemed to weigh how to begin. "Are we alone on this call?"

"Yes. See?" Sophia moved the laptop to the right and left to show no one else was in the room. "Now that I've confirmed it, can you tell me what this is all about?"

Alex leaned closer to the camera, clearly holding his stomach like he was going to be sick. "I know we only briefly met, ten years ago, but that trip to Comstock was the reason why I left Keystone."

"Why?"

"Because I just couldn't take the shit anymore. Everything he demanded. And for what?" Alex ran a hand over his thinning hair. "I've been living with this weight for so long. It might feel good to get it off my chest."

"Does this have something to do with Gina? Or with Evan Harlowe?"

Alex's face twisted with disgust. "If I never hear that man's name again, it'll be too soon."

The moment he'd said it, Sophia could tell he regretted it. "Don't worry. I have no use for him either."

"Has he blackmailed you as well?"

"Harlowe's been blackmailing you?" Sophia swallowed, studying her face on the screen to make sure it didn't reveal the surprise she felt inside. "Why?"

He let out a bitter laugh. "That's been the curse of this business for as long as I can remember. Half the people running Hollywood are on the rainbow spectrum, but no one is supposed to make that known. It's getting better, of course, but ten or fifteen years ago? It was worse than the military with the *don't ask, don't tell* bullshit."

Sophia nodded slowly. "Can you tell me exactly what happened between you and Professor Harlowe?"

Alex closed his eyes, massaging his temples. "Being a gay man working for a traditional family values corporation like Keystone was a risk. I knew that. But it was a good job, and I thought I'd been careful, you know? But that man, he has *friends* everywhere."

"Harlowe?" Regretting speaking the name aloud, Sophia held her breath as she waited for him to respond. The way Alex had said the word *friends*, it was clear he meant something more sinister.

"I suspect his spies were in a similar situation as I found myself in over the years. Evan Harlowe is a tricky bastard, with those good looks of his, dapper suits, and that magnetic personality. But he doesn't have friends. If he pretends otherwise, rest assured he has a purpose in mind for you."

"What did he have in mind for you?" Sophia asked, her body tensing.

Alex shook his head. "If I tell you, you'll hate me. I know neither of us works for Keystone anymore, but I'm in talks with an IBC affiliate. I hear you have clout there now."

"All the more reason to tell me," Sophia said soothingly. "I'm not like the professor in question. Whatever happened back then, I would never use it against you now. Does this have to do with Gina Mitchells?"

Alex's shoulders sagged. "I still feel guilty about that. The kind that claws at you." He twisted his shirt with a clenched fist.

"Because you flat out told Gina to give up screenwriting?" Sophia guessed.

He stared blankly into the camera before shame washed over his face. "I didn't even read her script because I didn't want to know how much damage I could be inflicting. Then, I heard IBC bought one, and everyone's been singing her praises." His upper body convulsed. "I didn't want to do it. Who was I to tell someone not to chase their dream? I was working in movies, and no one thought I could when I was her age. I hate that evil man and the things he makes you do."

"Why Gina?"

"He didn't want her to leave for LA, but he didn't want it to seem like he had anything to do with it, either. No fingerprints. That's how he put it."

"I don't think I follow. Why did he need a twenty-two-year-old so badly he was willing to ruin her career prospects, not to mention her personal life, over it?"

"Look; he's a decent filmmaker," Alex said, "but he's no Ken Burns. Oh, he got lucky with a couple things when he was young, but after that, rumor was he couldn't hack it on his own. He'd been relying on his students for years to keep him at all relevant, but when he got ahold of Gina, I think he felt he'd struck gold."

"She's very talented," Sophia said, anger burbling in her chest.

"And he's very manipulative. Not to mention lacking any moral compass. He called me up and told me if I didn't agree to meet with his protege the next time I came through the area, and tell her she had no chance in screenwriting, he was going to out me not only to Keystone but to my parents."

"How did he even know?"

"We were in college together." Alex gritted his teeth, his face turning scarlet. "I thought we were friends. But he filed it away, like he always does. Striking when it suits him. I know it might sound cowardly, but ten years ago, I hadn't come out to anyone. Not at work, not in my family. They thought

Larry was my roommate. I didn't know what to do. I was scared."

"That's understandable." Sophia thought of her own family, how accepting they'd been of her over the years. But she knew not everyone had such good fortune. Gina's own strained relationship with her family ever since coming out, after all, proved Sophia was lucky. "Being scared is a natural response, Alex. I get it. This was Harlowe's fault for using you."

"I've since learned I'm not the only one. There's a covert group of successful Hollywood insiders who have all been victimized by Harlowe over the years. We've wanted to rectify the damage we've inflicted at the devil's behest, but we don't know how."

A light bulb clicked in Sophia's head. "Is that why you're telling me now? Because you and others want to come out of the Harlowe victim closet?"

"I don't know. The truth is I've been sick all morning, waiting for Larry to get this call." Alex looked on the verge of tears. "I mean, even now, that vile man has me doing his bidding out of guilt, getting my own husband to be in this documentary because he assured me it would be a way of making amends to Gina for what I did."

Sophia spoke quickly, her heart pounding as a plan began to form in her mind. "Alex, I hate to tell you this, but Harlowe is doing everything he can to undermine Gina. He has no intention of giving her any credit for this film, no matter what he told her. But I think I have a way to turn the tables, if you're willing to help."

"Anything," he confirmed, striking a fist against his palm. "Harlowe claims to be a champion of the underdog. Women, people of color, the LGBTQ+ community. He's none of those. If you have a way to expose him for the monster he is, you can count me in."

CHAPTER NINETEEN

Gina stood at the edge of the common, staring at the gazebo. It was evening, but the sun hadn't yet set, having reached that time of year when it remained light well past the dinner hour. The warm spring breeze and abundant flowers were even more at odds than ever with the Christmas decorations that covered every surface.

One more week, and then filming would be done. After that? Gina wasn't sure.

Especially now.

Grasping her phone from her pocket, Gina tried for the millionth time not to panic over Sophia's text message.

We have to talk.

Seriously, did the woman know no other ways to phrase things so as not to provoke an aneurysm?

While the last time Gina had received a text like

this, it had turned out okay in the end, it was difficult for her to see how her luck would hold out. Taking Sophia up on her offer to help today had been a bad idea. It was too much to ask, and Sophia would be well within her rights to call Gina out on it.

Or, worse.

Given the stress she was under, what would she do if Sophia changed her mind about their relationship? The film was nearly done, and they were a week away from the Pride Festival. They hadn't discussed what the future would look like after that. A challenge, that was for sure, even under the best of circumstances. And if the issue with Professor Harlowe had demonstrated anything, it was how far from perfect the circumstances really were. But surely that couldn't be what this was about.

Couldn't it, though?

Gina felt faint. Was it possible to simply ignore the message? That was her preferred method of dealing with shitty situations. Just keep paddling like hell, avoiding the rocks in the river, and turning a blind eye to the whitewater on the horizon. Avoid, and hold on for dear life.

That was exactly what had caused their relationship to crash and burn the first time.

Sighing, Gina headed toward the gazebo where she could already see Sophia waiting. Time to face the music.

Sophia was seated when Gina arrived, and it

occurred to her that benches had been added since the last time they were here. That would've been convenient. Gina's knees had been bruised for a week.

Now is not the time to be thinking about that.

"Hey." Gina stood beside the bench but didn't sit, not wanting to get too close and potentially place herself in the middle of danger.

"Hey, yourself." Sophia's expression softened as if detecting Gina's *heading to the guillotine* vibes. "Are you okay?"

"You tell me." Gina held up her phone. "I came away unscathed the first time you sent me a text like this, but…?"

"You might want to sit down." Sophia motioned to the bench beside her. Gina lowered herself onto it, her spirits sinking as quickly as her body.

"It's *sit down* bad?" *Just flipping fantastic.* Gina rocked back and forth on the bench, unable to still the chaos that was racing through every cell.

In a move that was the opposite of what Gina had expected, Sophia eased close enough to wrap an arm around her shoulders. "I learned something today, and while I know the news is going to be upsetting to you, given our past history of letting things stay secret and come between us—I decided it's best for us to talk it through this time, instead of avoiding it."

"I like avoiding," Gina mumbled, although the tension in her shoulders was starting to lessen as she realized this was not about their future together, as she'd feared. No, that difficult conversation could be saved for another day.

"I'm aware," Sophia said with a laugh, giving Gina a nudge with her shoulder. "However, this is something we need to tackle head-on, together."

"Together?"

"Absolutely. Always." Sophia threaded her fingers with Gina's.

Gina let out a relieved sigh. "This really isn't about us?"

"Not exactly." The hesitation in Sophia's words didn't do Gina's mental health any favors.

"I feel like I need tequila shots to get through this."

"More like a punching bag to get your anger out."

Gina repositioned, sitting with her back against the hard wooden railing of the gazebo for support. "Hit me with it."

"It's about Harlowe."

Gina's forehead creased, but she didn't say anything. Sophia looked like she would rather walk through fire than say whatever it was that she needed to get off her chest.

"I don't know how else to say this, but the guy's toxic."

"I know he can be demanding—"

"That's the least of it." Sophia slanted her head, meaning she meant business, and Gina had to listen.

Gina's body clenched, but she didn't do anything to

stop Sophia from continuing. In fact, what she really needed was to get it over with.

Sophia laid out everything she'd learned since Gina had left seven hours earlier. Blackmail. Coercion. Those were just the tip of the iceberg when it came to the treachery Sophia laid out. When she'd finished her tale, Gina's brain swam in the overwhelming evidence of just how douchey Dr. Harlowe could be.

"You spoke to *eight* people Harlowe screwed over? Since breakfast?"

Sophia nodded. "I'm trying to get into contact with a handful of others."

Gina stared above Sophia's head, contemplating the Christmas garland on a nearby lamppost, wondering if blending into the fake snow on the bushes was an option. "I don't know—how do I process all of this?"

"Slowly," Sophia recommended.

"But... I made life decisions based on my conversation with Alex Cross. I ended our relationship because of it. You're telling me, it was because Harlowe didn't want me to move to LA? All so I could continue to prop up his flagging career?"

Sophia appeared on the verge of tears. "It seems so."

"And he threatened to out Alex? Even to his parents?" Gina knew what it was like to lose family over coming out. Anyone who would inflict that on another person wasn't just a *bad* guy. Only a heinous villain would behave that way.

Sophia nodded. "Yes, he did."

"What kind of human being does something like that? He's always claimed to be a champion of marginalized people, but he was using that against people." Gina cradled her head with both palms as if needing to keep her head from exploding. Rage swirled inside her, hot and thick like smoke from an inferno. "I can't process this. I don't understand how anyone could do such a thing. For something so stupid. He wrecked careers. Lives. For what?"

"Pride," Sophia replied.

"I feel helpless, and I don't like it." Gina balled her fists. "What am I supposed to do with this information?"

The question was mostly rhetorical, but to her surprise, Sophia spoke up. "I have an idea, but you might not like it."

"Does it involve punching him in the face?" Gina smacked a fist into her other hand. "I've never been violent, but I'm willing to give it a try."

"While I'd love to see that, I have something else in mind. Something that will hit him where it really hurts."

"Where's that?"

"His pride, of course." Sophia's eyes twinkled, and while Gina wasn't sure she was following entirely, she sensed there was a double meaning to the words. "But we don't have a lot of time. If you're on board with it, we're going to need to call in some help."

Intrigued, Gina asked, "Help from whom?"

"Ken Abrams, the head of entertainment at IBC."

This still didn't make the plan clear, but the way Sophia's face lit up with an almost evil glee, Gina trusted it would be worthwhile.

"From what I know, Ken loves ratings, and what I have in mind will be a ratings bonanza. But, before I reach out, I want to ensure you're okay with taking Harlowe down."

Without a moment of hesitation, Gina nodded her assent. "I want to take the bastard down."

Sophia didn't waste a second, punching at her phone like a possessed woodpecker. "Ken? It's Sophia Rossi. I need your help with something big."

CHAPTER TWENTY

THE SUN BEAT DOWN ON SOPHIA'S BACK AS the rainbow float she was riding on made its way through the center of downtown Comstock. The crowd that lined the sidewalks waved Pride flags, and several people were calling out her name. She glanced down at the Grand Marshal banner she wore across her chest like a beauty pageant queen. Reaching into a large plastic bag beside her, Sophia grabbed a handful of candy and tossed it into the crowd, eliciting a roar.

"This is unreal," Sophia said to Jill Davidson, who was beside her on the float. She was nearly yelling to be heard above the noise. "They're acting like I'm the queen or something."

"You are the Queen of Christmas, after all," Jill said, flinging more candy to the onlookers. "And a hometown hero. People like to believe their dreams can come true, and you're living proof."

"I'm finally feeling that way." Sophia fanned the back of her neck as beads of sweat trickled down her skin. "I'm just grateful I don't have to be dressed like a Christmas queen for this parade. It feels like the Fourth of July. If I never have to wear another parka in the summer again, I'd be happy."

"Please don't tell me that's a deal breaker." Jill's tone suggested she was saying this for a reason.

Sophia turned a sharp look on her companion. "Why is that?"

"I might have some news." Jill continued waving to the crowd, not losing sight of their mission. "IBC is thrilled with how *Christmas at Rainbow Falls* is turning out."

"They'd better be," Sophia joked. "We took Dix's steaming pile of dog excrement and turned it into gold with Gina's script and Hattie Dandrige."

"On time and on budget, no less." Jill threw candy to the crowd with unbridled exuberance. "I can't believe we actually wrapped filming last night. I was sure we'd run over by a week, at least."

"I told you, four weeks is a luxury." Sophia cast a sideways glance at Jill. "So, what's this news you thought you might have for me?"

Jill grinned. "IBC wants to offer you a multi-picture deal."

"Multiple Christmas movies?" Sophia guessed, suddenly understanding why her confession about wearing winter clothing in hot weather might have given the executive producer cause for concern. "I take it they'll be filming over the summer months."

"More than likely," Jill admitted. "Filming in Massachusetts was amazing for the tax credits, but you know Keystone does all of theirs in Canada for a reason."

"Cheaper labor, wintery scenery, experienced crew," Sophia listed a few out of the many. "I guess I'm lucky I haven't sold my condo in Vancouver yet."

"Your luck's even better than that," Jill said, unable to conceal the excitement in her voice. "IBC wants to move beyond just Christmas. We're thinking a mystery series with you as the star. Think Jessica Fletcher meets Miss Fisher, but with a sexy lesbian as the amateur sleuth."

"Sexy lesbian, huh?" Sophia tossed two handfuls of candy into the air like they were confetti, laughing as kids—and more than a few adults—scampered into the street to grab the pieces.

"I thought that would get your attention. And hopefully it makes up for having to pretend to be freezing all summer while trying not to swat mosquitoes and sweating through your wool coat and mittens."

"Honestly? That sounds amazing." For a change of pace, Sophia threw rainbow beads as the float turned down the stretch of road that would take them along the edge of the Comstock College campus. As her alma mater came into view,

Sophia's eyes filled with tears. Was this all a dream?

"Don't cry yet," Jill urged. "I haven't even told you the best part. Are you ready?"

Sophia pressed a hand to her chest. "I don't know if I can take more good news. Not in this heat."

Jill shrugged. "Okay. It can wait."

"Mean!" Sophia teased, laughing as she pretended to give Jill's shoulder a slug. "Tell me. I absolutely can *not* wait another second."

Before Jill could answer, a screaming horde of college students performed a cheer of sorts in Sophia's honor.

Jill said to Sophia, "I bet when you were in high school, you never thought you'd be a gay icon."

Yes, but at what cost? No. She couldn't let herself think like that. Yes, she and Gina had missed out on that time together—no thanks to Professor Harlowe's evil meddling—but they would have so many more years together. Focusing on the past would only bring sadness. Sophia was done with sadness. No more crying on Christmas, exhausted and lonely.

The parade came to an end in front of the towering iron gates that marked the main entrance to the campus. Gina's student Megan helped Jill and Sophia down from the float. As soon as Jill's feet hit the ground, she said goodbye with a wave, heading off toward a row of vendor tents that had been set up on the college's central quad. Sophia couldn't blame her.

The smell of carnival style snacks wafted through the air like a whiff of heaven itself.

"Where's Gina?" Sophia asked, looking all around for her girlfriend and coming up empty. "If I so much as consider grabbing a cotton candy without her, she'll kill me."

"She had to take care of some last-minute business before the film premiere," Megan explained. "She said she'd catch up as soon as she could. In the meantime—"

"There's my baby!" Sophia's mom squealed, rushing at her with the rest of Sophia's family in tow.

"—your mom was looking for you," Megan finished, not that it was necessary.

Her mom had screamed so loudly Sophia had instinctively raised her shoulders to protect her ears.

"I just remembered I have somewhere else to be." With that, Megan turned tail and fled.

"Coward," Sophia whispered, wishing she could do the same. "Mom—dear God, Bella! Are you going to have that baby *today*?"

Bella stared daggers at Sophia. "If one more person cracks a labor joke, I'm going to punch them. Got me?" She pointed her finger in Sophia's face, shifting it to her sister Carrie, her father, and her mother in turn. "Dad, let's find some shade, okay?"

"Of course, my Belladonna," he said indulgently.

"I wasn't kidding about the whole labor thing, though," Sophia said once the coast was clear.

"The baby's two days late already." Carrie hefted her shoulders. "I think all of us will be relieved when it comes."

"As long as it's not in the middle of the festival." Sophia grimaced.

"Do you know what we need, ladies?" Sophia's mom asked.

"A puppy?" Sophia pressed her palms together in supplication, Carrie quickly joining in. "Please?"

"Yes, yes. I know," their mom said in that pained way of hers, not because she had regrets, aside from the fact her daughters were taller and older, making it harder to inspire fear in them. "I was such a terrible mom because we never had a dog."

"I would have walked it every day," Sophia stated emphatically.

"I would have fed it," Carrie added with a pout.

"And, I'm the Queen of England," their mother retorted. "No more guilt trips about puppies, or I won't buy you any fried dough."

Both Sophia and Carrie mimed zipping their lips shut.

Their mom's expression grew smug. "That's what I thought."

The three of them crossed the lush green lawn, swiveling their heads to take in all the popup tents that lined the edges. Each one was filled with more rainbow-covered merchandise than Sophia had ever seen. But she'd have to come back through later for a closer look. As the breeze stirred, there was something else that had her full attention.

Sophia stopped, taking a deep breath so full of sugar and butter she could taste it in the air. "What's that smell?"

"Kettle corn," Carrie answered.

"Fried dough and kettle corn." Sophia let out a long, contented sigh. "You can't get more New England than that. I think I'm in heaven."

"You do seem unusually happy today. What gives?" Carrie studied her sister's face like she was trying to figure out a riddle.

"It's Pride." Sophia wasn't going to share the good news she'd received from Jill until she had a chance to tell Gina. "I was on a float, and I guess I'm still floating."

"Man, that was corny." Carrie nudged Sophia's side with an elbow. "It's a good thing Gina writes your dialogue."

"It really is," Sophia agreed.

The way the movie worked out, Gina would be penning many more screenplays. The timing of her success couldn't have been better. Considering what Gina was about to orchestrate, there seemed little chance the tenure committee would vote to approve her request. If anything, they were likely to seek her resignation.

There was bravery, and there was Gina.

She was also speed-walking toward Sophia, waving at her with both arms to get her attention.

"There you are!" Gina wrapped an arm around Sophia's waist. "You were zoned out there for a second. Everything okay?"

"Just fine," Sophia assured her, noticing the lines around Gina's eyes that indicated she was a lot more stressed than she was letting on.

"You're just in time," Sophia's mom chimed in. "I'm buying fried dough."

"This is pretty much the best day ever, isn't it?" Sophia said, hoping to put Gina at ease with a kiss to her cheek.

While Sophia's mom and sister waited in line, she turned to Gina. "Did you get everything you needed to the AV department?"

Gina answered with a nod.

"How are you holding up?" Sophia gave Gina's arm a squeeze.

"I just want it to be over with." Gina's voice was low and shaky, and Sophia wondered how close Gina was to throwing up. If Sophia had been in the same position, she would've done so by now, for sure.

"I know, sweetheart," Sophia soothed. "Soon. In another few hours, Harlowe will get his well-deserved comeuppance."

"My career will crash and burn, right alongside his." Gina's expression was grim but determined. As they'd discussed dozens of times in the past week since Sophia had suggested the plan, it was a necessary risk. No amount of job security was worth letting a monster like Gina's professor continue to prey on the defenseless as he had for so many years.

Sophia was on the verge of telling Gina about the conversation she'd had with Jill on the float, but one of the students from the Pride committee flagged Gina down.

"I've gotta run," Gina said apologetically.

"What about your fried dough?" Sophia's mom asked, returning to where they'd been standing, carrying several paper baskets of the steaming, powdered sugar covered confections.

"Can I take it to go?" Gina offered a grateful smile as Sophia's mom handed her one of the containers. "Thanks, Angie."

"Good luck," Sophia called as Gina headed toward the college's auditorium, where final preparations were going on for the big event. Her stomach tightened as Gina turned and waved. "See you inside."

CHAPTER TWENTY-ONE

The auditorium was packed, and Gina suspected it had more to do with the thousand-dollar raffle prize than anyone dying to see a teaser of Harlowe's documentary. Not that he wasn't doing his best to ingratiate himself to every single person in the room, conveniently forgetting he hadn't created this self-proclaimed masterpiece as a solo project.

Not that it mattered. By the time the night was over, Gina hoped everyone would forget she'd ever had anything to do with the despicable man.

"Gina, come here." Harlowe motioned for her to join him where he stood with several college administration bigwigs, looking like a turkey getting ready to dazzle everyone with his tail feathers. "This is my assistant, Gina. I wouldn't have gotten this far without her. She makes the best cup of espresso." Professor Harlowe laughed, but Gina was relieved to see his two companions, who both knew full well she was an assistant *professor*, and not his glorified errand girl, didn't join in. "I'm kidding, of course."

The lights flickered. Gina couldn't help but notice the relief on both men's faces as they knew their time chatting with Harlowe was nearly over. How had Gina missed the looks in the eyes of people dealing with Harlowe all these years? Now, she'd never be able to unsee them.

"It's time to find your seats for my masterpiece. We'll talk investment opportunities after, gentlemen. Still plenty of time to get in on the ground floor. This one has Sundance accolades written all over it." Harlowe was patting himself on the back so much Gina suspected he must be a contortionist. There was no doubt he was counting the money these guys would dole out after the teaser. Hell, he'd probably already chosen the spot on the shelf to display those awards he expected to win.

"I have a good feeling about this," he said, only addressing Gina directly now that the more important people had gone.

"It's going to knock everyone's socks off," Gina predicted. That much was guaranteed, though not in the way he believed.

The lights dimmed.

Sophia appeared by Gina's side, holding her hand as they stood pressed together in the packed auditorium. The screen lit up, but instead of the anticipated documentary, Amanda Morgan appeared on the screen.

"Hello, Comstock!" the renowned nighttime anchorwoman spoke to the audience via a live stream from IBC's New York studio. The audience tittered with surprise, clearly thinking this was all part of the regular schedule of events. "I can't tell you how honored I am to be here with you tonight."

Harlowe whipped his head around, searching for Gina. When he caught sight of her, his face was the picture of confusion.

Not fear. Not yet. But that would come soon enough.

Gripping Sophia's arm a little tighter, Gina gave her one-time mentor a knowing smile, one she hoped would haunt him in his dreams.

"Most of you know Professor Harlowe. He's one of the few male professors on your campus, so he probably sticks out like a sore thumb, always dressed like a proper gentleman."

More laughter from the crowd. The professor was certainly well-known for his bow ties and vests. He was possibly the only man Gina had ever met who wore a seersucker suit in the summer without a trace of irony.

"Here's the thing," Amanda continued. "You don't know him like I now do, after conducting twelve interviews with some of Harlowe's associates. Well, that word isn't quite right. I think the better word is *victims*, and once you've heard what I have, I think you'll agree. Shall we get started?" As an uneasy silence descended over the room, Amanda rubbed her hands together in a mixture of anticipation and glee. The screen went a little fuzzy, while the pre-recorded interview segment began to play.

Take down was probably a better term for it.

Gina couldn't help but feel awe at what could be accomplished in only a week with a powerhouse like Amanda Morgan on the job, and the full blessing and resources of IBC behind her.

Simply amazing.

"Kyle—and, I should say, we're not using your real name to protect you—can I ask, how did you meet Evan Harlowe?" Amanda directed this question at an unassuming man in his late fifties with thick spectacles.

"We grew up together," Kyle replied, pulling his hat lower as if afraid to be found out despite the crew's efforts to keep his face mostly in shadow.

Amanda offered a warm, encouraging smile that immediately seemed to put him at ease. "How far back?"

"Kindergarten." The man's body slumped with sadness.

"That's a long time."

"It is." Kyle shifted his gaze downward, his shoulders stooped like the burden of whatever he was about to share was weighing him down.

"When did he start blackmailing you?" Amanda asked gently.

Instantly, Harlowe lunged out of his chair, screaming, "Shut it off! Shut it off!"

Gina tensed, suddenly on the defensive. Even so, she couldn't deny the burst of triumph that shot through her when Harlowe raced toward the back of the auditorium.

Megan, Destiny, and Kayla stood in the aisle, blocking the professor from getting anywhere near the AV booth. Gina had arranged this with the students in advance, having anticipated this would be Harlowe's first move.

The man on the screen paused, as if he too had anticipated the outburst. He adjusted his hat, before saying, "Not until he needed something."

"What did he need?"

"Talent." Despite his obvious discomfort, Kyle let out a little laugh at his joke, an endearing move that seemed to highlight both his sincerity and his humanity. "I'd made a documentary when I was fresh out of college, but I couldn't sell it. Evan had contacts, so we joined forces. That is until he decided he wanted to take all the credit."

"Why?"

"He's always thought he was better than everyone else. But he reached a point where he needed everyone else to believe it, too."

Her heart beating faster, Gina whispered into

Sophia's ear, "Is he saying Harlowe didn't make his *first* documentary himself?"

Equally wide-eyed, Sophia nodded that this was her understanding, too.

Gina had heard some of the horror stories, but once Ken Abrams had looped in Amanda Morgan to do the exposé, the project had been out of her hands. She was seeing the final result along with the rest of the audience for the very first time. If she'd had any doubt Evan Harlowe would be ruined after this, it was gone now.

He'd be a pariah. And so would she, no doubt, for having worked side by side with him for so long. It wasn't fair, but she'd come to terms with it the best she could. When a great man fell, it was always the women around him who got blamed for not knowing more, sooner.

At least she could take pleasure in knowing, in the end, she'd been the one to wield the ax.

"Why didn't you expose Professor Harlowe as the fraud he is?" Amanda asked. "After all, that film went on to win several prestigious awards. They should've been yours."

Kyle's cheeks blushed crimson. "Because he had something I didn't want to get out, and he said if I breathed a word about the documentary, he'd release… the thing."

"By talking to me, though, you're risking that he still might."

"I know." The man covered his face. "I know, but after I heard how many other people had been blackmailed by Evan, I had to speak up."

At this point, Harlowe tried to push his way past the Pride committee, but they stood firm, not letting him force his way through.

"What did he have?" Amanda continued.

In an instant, the man's face went from red to almost a greenish hue. "One summer, when we were teenagers, Evan had a party at his house, and I hooked up with someone... a man... and Evan—he got it on video."

"Evan Harlowe filmed you having sex and kept the tape?"

The crowd gasped, and it was difficult to hear Kyle's reply of yes.

"How long did he have it until he threatened you?"

"Five years." Kyle blinked rapidly. "By this point, I was engaged to my wife, and I simply couldn't bear... She didn't know I was bi then..." The rest of his answer faded into sobs.

"He waited five years to tell you about its existence?" Amanda asked when Kyle had regained some composure.

"Yes. He waited until he needed something from me. We'd both been film nerds. We dreamed of becoming famous directors. And then, Evan did."

"It was your first film that launched Dr. Harlowe's career."

"Yes. It was also my last film. I never had the stomach for it again after that."

"He's lying!" Harlowe screamed, but security was arriving through a side door, and the president of the college was directing them to where the professor stood. Gina was frozen in place, watching like it was all part of a movie being filmed around her. This couldn't be happening, could it? As they dragged him out of the auditorium, Harlowe continued screaming, "Lies. It's all lies!"

"I need air," Gina whispered to Sophia, her throat tight.

They left the auditorium together. Outside, Gina bent over, her hands on her knees.

"You okay?" Sophia asked, placing a hand gently on Gina's back.

"I might be sick." In truth, as soon as she said this out loud, she started to feel better, stronger. A moment later, Gina straightened. "How did I not see him for who he was?"

"He's very charming and cunning." There was no judgment in Sophia's eyes or tone, though Gina harbored plenty of it toward herself in her own heart.

"B-but..." Gina could only shake her head, letting the truth wash over her. She'd been used. The man had never blackmailed her, but he'd manipulated her nonetheless, all the while making her think he was an ally. She wasn't sure which was a bigger betrayal, hers or Kyle's.

"Professor Mitchells!" As one of the women from the tenure review committee approached, Gina saw her academic life flash before her eyes.

This was it, the end of her career. Gina straightened herself to her full height, lifting her chin. If she was going to go down with this ship, she would do it with dignity. "Dr. Miriam, I would like to apologize—"

"What on earth for?" The woman's response was swift and surprisingly fierce, and it seemed to Gina she was looking for someone to kick in the shins, or possibly the balls, and experiencing grave disappointment that no one in the immediate vicinity fit the bill. "Harlowe's the asshole, not you."

At this point, some people started to stream out of the auditorium, looking dazed. Gina couldn't blame them. She felt the same.

"Even so," Gina said, "I know this type of theatrics might reflect poorly on the college. That wasn't my intention."

"I couldn't give a damn." Dr. Miriam chuckled, presumably because of what Gina knew must be a look of utter shock on her face. "Between you and me, I never liked Harlowe. I couldn't understand why so many of my peers here at the college fawned over him like a demi-god. If I'm being completely honest, seeing him brought down like that, and by Amanda Morgan, no less? It added ten years to my life."

"It did?" For the first time since she and Sophia had hatched this plan, Gina began to consider that she might not be sacrificed on the funeral pyre of her mentor's career.

"We need to talk about some things," Dr. Miriam said. "Including your upcoming tenure review, but it's safe to say it's a lock now. I wouldn't be surprised if you end up taking over the department sooner than we anticipated."

"You anticipated… me?" Gina's head spun. She'd had no clue anyone had been considering her for such a role, even way down the line. If there had been rumors, Professor Harlowe sure as hell had never let on.

"Now, if you'll excuse me, I want to see the rest of that film." With that, the woman went back inside the auditorium.

"Head of the department?" Gina had to say it out loud, and even after she had, she couldn't believe it.

"Wow." Sophia's mouth stayed open, forming an O for a long second before morphing into a grin. Grabbing Gina's hands, she hopped up and down. "You did it. You got what you wanted!"

"I… I did… I guess." If that was the case, why did Gina feel so numb?

Sensing it immediately, Sophia asked, "What's wrong?"

The reality hit her like a blow to the stomach, and it took everything Gina had not to double over. "We're right back where we were."

"What do you mean?" Sophia put on a brave face, but she wasn't fooling Gina.

"Ten years ago. Me, staying on the east coast. You, heading to Hollywood."

"There's a big difference, now," Sophia assured her in a tone that was soft but firm.

"What?" There was a pleading quality to the question. If Sophia had an answer, Gina needed to know.

"We're older now, and we both know what we want."

Gina's heart pounded. "Which is?"

"Each other." It sounded so simple Gina almost believed that was all there was.

Almost.

"The distance, though," she began, but Sophia was already shaking her head.

"Yes, it will suck. Not gonna lie. But it will only be for the summers."

Gina frowned. "What do you mean? I thought for sure, once the film wrapped, IBC would be offering you a massive new contract."

"Well, they did. Christmas movies filming in Canada over the summer, plus a cozy mystery series that would run the rest of the year." Sophia bit her lower lip, indecision seeming to weigh on her for a moment. "I've decided I'm only interested in the Christmas part. The rest of the time, I want to be here. With you."

"When did this...? Why didn't you tell me?" Gina's

thoughts raced as she tried to process what was happening. One thing stood out. She couldn't let Sophia make that sacrifice. "No, you can't give up the series. That's too much."

"It is not." Sophia had that look on her face that said *don't you dare argue*. Gina knew she'd learned it from Mrs. Rossi, and she would no sooner cross the daughter in this mood than she would the mother. "Ten years ago, you took my choice away from me. I won't let you do that now. It's my decision to make, and I choose you. That's all there is to it."

"Not so fast," Gina heard herself saying, suddenly breaking free of the stupor she'd been in since leaving the auditorium. "I was already prepared to lose my job tonight at the college, and become *persona non grata* in academia as a whole because of my association with Harlowe. You know what? I was at peace with it. This news about tenure doesn't change that."

"Gina," Sophia spoke in barely a whisper, "it's what you've worked for all these years."

"No, it's my job," Gina corrected, the passion building in her chest as she spoke. "A life with you is my dream. I was ready to pack up and head to LA with you before I spoke with Dr. Miriam, and I'm still ready to do it now. Nothing has changed."

"Do you mean that?" Sophia began to tremble visibly, and Gina rushed to pull her into a tight embrace.

"Absolutely." Gina's cheeks grew moist with tears

as she held Sophia like she'd never let go. In fact, she had no intention of ever doing so. Not this time.

"Hey, you two. Get a room." Jill laughed as Gina and Sophia jumped apart. "Are you celebrating the good news about the IBC contract?"

Sophia cleared her throat. "I... that is, I'm not exactly sure about that contract, Jill." Gina opened her mouth to protest, but Sophia held up a hand to stop her. "It's just that going back to LA seems like such—"

"Back to LA?" Jill frowned. "Why would you be going back to LA? I thought you wanted to do the mystery series."

"Yes, I do, but..." It was Sophia's turn to look confused. Gina, too, was puzzled.

Jill's eyes widened. "Oh goodness. Didn't I mention? The mystery series is filming in Massachusetts. Not Sholan Falls, though. Closer to the coast. You'll be on the east coast, not west."

"It's here?" Sophia broke into a grin. "I'd be living here? You mean, Gina could keep teaching at Comstock?"

"Of course," Jill said, shifting her eyes to Gina. "There's Canada, but that's in the summer. Professors get summers off, right?"

Unable to speak, Gina nodded.

"Have you spent a summer in Canada? You're going to love it." Jill paused, a calculating look coming over her. "Although, I wanted to talk to you about something."

"Oh?" Gina's stomach tightened.

"It's this mystery series. I think you'd make an excellent addition to the writing team, if you'd like to give it a shot. It's going to require some snappy dialogue, and your style suits it perfectly. You'd stay busy, but you should be able to fit it in with your teaching schedule."

"I'll make certain of it." Gina pressed her hand to her chest, her heart beating against it like a kettle drum.

"Great job tonight, Gina," Jill said before wandering away, leaving Gina and Sophia alone.

"Were you really willing to give up the series for me?" Gina asked, holding her breath as she waited for Sophia to answer. She didn't have to wait long.

"Of course, I was. I told you I'm not going to lose you again. I would've stayed ten years ago, and I sure as heck wasn't going to leave you now." Sophia took a deep breath, a shyness settling over her features. "But, would you really have left everything you've worked for behind and moved across the country just to be with me?"

"Do you even have to ask?" Gina swallowed a lump that formed in her throat as she thought back to their graduation day. "Ten years ago, I made the biggest mistake of my life. I let someone I shouldn't have trusted make me think I couldn't make it on my own. In a way, Harlowe was right about that, but it wasn't him I needed. It was you. I know that now. I would follow you to the ends of the earth if that's what it took."

Sophia giggled, her eyes shining with joyful tears. "As it happens, neither one of us is going anywhere. Just wait until my mom finds out."

Gina reached for Sophia, pulling her as close as she could, until it felt like they had merged into one. "Am I crazy, or does it seem like everything is finally working out for us?"

Sophia chuckled. "Isn't it about damn time?"

Celebrate love with the I Heart SapphFic Pride Collection, eight standalone romances offering a taste of the very best modern sapphic fiction has to offer.

Be sure to subscribe to I Heart SapphFic to discover the latest in sapphic fiction every week! Because love is love, and everyone deserves a happily ever after.

IHeartSapphFic.com

IF YOU ENJOYED Gina and Sophia's story but wish you could see the movie they were filming, we have some great news! TB Markinson and Miranda MacLeod will be releasing *Christmas at Rainbow Falls*, a feel-good holiday romance with all the gingerbread cookies, pine garland, and Christmas movie vibes you could possibly ask for, in November 2022.

And as a special surprise, there will be a bonus chapter with Sophia and Gina attending a Hollywood premiere of their film included at the end of the book!

Subscribe to I Heart SapphFic to stay up to date on all the sapphic fiction new releases, including *Christmas at Rainbow Falls*, or keep reading to find out how to subscribe to TB and Miranda's newsletters and receive your free ebook bonus gifts.

A HUGE THANK YOU!

If you've read some of our other books, you might have recognized a few cameo appearances from characters you've met before! Jill Davidson was a supporting character in Miranda's book, *Love's Encore*, and you can find Amanda Morgan's journey to true love in our Golden Crown Literary Society Award's finalist for best romance, *The AM Show*.

Now that we've cowritten so many books, we're often asked how we manage to work so well together. What many don't realize is Miranda and TB go way back. How far back? We were actually born in the same hospital, just nine weeks apart. While we may quibble about plot points, we're often laughing as we do.

For example, just the other day, Miranda said to TB, "Do you remember the time I told you not to eat that mud pie, and you did anyway and made yourself

A HUGE THANK YOU!

sick? You should have trusted me then, just like you should trust me now."

TB would like it noted that she hates dirt, and it wasn't the type of mud pie kids make on a playground, but the dessert consisting of ice cream, Oreo crust, fudge, and lots of chocolate. Miranda would like it noted this didn't happen when they were kids. It was two weeks ago. And TB is still complaining her belly hurts.

If you enjoyed *Take Two*, we would really appreciate a review on Amazon, Goodreads, or your favorite book review site. Even short reviews help immensely.

TB has published more than twenty-five novels, and she still finds it simply amazing people read her stories. When she hit publish on her first book back in 2013, she had no idea what would happen. It's been a wonderful journey, and she wouldn't be where she is today without your support.

If you want to stay in touch with TB, sign up for her newsletter. She'll send you a free copy of *A Woman Lost*, book 1 in the A Woman Lost series, plus the bonus chapters and Tropical Heat (a short story), all of which are exclusive to subscribers. And, you'll be able to enter monthly giveaways to win one of her books.

You'll also be one of the firsts to hear about her many misadventures, like the time she accidentally ordered thirty pounds of oranges, instead of five. To be honest, that stuff happens to TB a lot, which explains why she owns three of the exact same Nice Tits T-shirt. In case you're wondering, the shirt has pictures of the different tits of the bird variety because she has some pride.

Here's the link to join: http://eepurl.com/hhBhXX

And, if you want to follow Miranda, sign up for her newsletter. Subscribers will receive her first book, *Telling Lies Online*, for free. Also, she runs monthly giveaways, including paperbacks, ebooks, and audio, that her readers love. For cat fans, she shares adorable photos of her felines, who are sisters and tag-team to destroy everything in Miranda's house. Their first Christmas was a particularly trying time, and about half of the ornaments survived. Luckily, they're adorable. Seriously, you don't want to miss out on Miranda's heartfelt and funny newsletters. Here's the link to join: mirandamacleod.com/list

Thanks again for reading Take Two. It's because of you that we are able to follow our dreams of being writers. It's a wonderful gift, and we appreciate each and every reader.

TB & Miranda

ABOUT THE AUTHORS

TB Markinson is an American who's recently returned to the US after a seven-year stint in the UK and Ireland. When she isn't writing, she's traveling the world, watching sports on the telly, visiting pubs in New England, or reading. Not necessarily in that order.

Visit TB's website (lesbianromancesbytbm.com) to say hello. On the *Lesbians Who Write* weekly podcast, she and Clare Lydon dish about the good, the bad, and the ugly of writing.

Originally from southern California, Miranda MacLeod now lives in New England and writes heartfelt romances and romantic comedies featuring witty and charmingly flawed women that you'll want to marry. Or just grab a coffee with, if that's more your thing.

Before becoming a writer, she spent way too many years in graduate school, worked in professional theater and film, and held temp jobs in just about every office building in downtown Boston. To find out about her upcoming releases, be sure to sign up for her mailing list at mirandamacleod.com.

TB and Miranda also co-own *I Heart SapphFic*, a website for authors and readers of sapphic fiction to stay up-to-date on all the latest sapphic fiction news.

Printed in Great Britain
by Amazon